Praise for *IN THE LIGHT OF YOU*

"[A] raw, blistering coming-of-age novel . . . Singer evokes with rare passion the tumultuous confusions and conflicts as teens seek to work out their racial and sexual identities. . . . Readers will find Mikal's erratic passage through a rough adolescence both vivid and compelling."
—*Publishers Weekly*

"In furiously fast-paced prose . . . Singer vivifies the attraction of the white power movement, drawing both the long, boring stretches spent playing video games and the heated moments of violence, set against a backdrop of sex and metal music. . . . Singer's percussive prose [works] its magic. An unblinking portrait of young white rage."
—*Booklist*

"Quite simply, *In the Light of You* is one of the finest coming-of-age novels published so far this century. Incendiary and moving, deeply relevant and searingly honest, it deserves to catapult Nathan Singer to the top of the list of America's best young novelists."
—John Connolly, *New York Times* bestselling author of *The Book of Lost Things*

"With prose brutal as a tumble through barbed wire and a tweaker's furious energy, Nathan Singer has crafted a chilling look inside the white power movement. A riveting story of hatred, fear, longing, and maybe, just possibly, redemption."

—Marcus Sakey, *Wall Street Journal* bestselling author of *The Blade Itself*

"Haunting, raw, and with an unexpected punch of redemption, Nathan Singer's *In the Light of You* can leave no one in doubt that he is the heir apparent to Hubert Selby Jr. Singer's electric prose is impossible to walk away from and will stay with you long after you've finished the last page."

—Tasha Alexander, *New York Times* bestselling author of *And Only to Deceive*

"Raw and beautiful . . . The world Singer creates is seamlessly authentic, and Mikal is the kind of complicated, flawed, and completely compelling character that very few writers could pull off. Singer's prose is as stark and brutal as the world he describes, but it's also riveting. . . . It carries the kind of redemptive power that reminds us why we read novels in the first place."

—*In Denver Times*

"Visceral . . . one of those rare novels that works on numerous levels, and in addition to succeeding as a cautionary tale about intolerance and discrimination, it's also a chilling exploration into the psyche of those involved in America's racist underground, as well as an acerbic commentary on the overall depraved state of the planet's (allegedly) most advanced species. Blending the gratuitous violence of *A Clockwork Orange* and rhetoric of Adolf Hitler's *Mein Kampf* with a surreal sense of naiveté à la *The Catcher in the Rye*, Singer brilliantly utilizes contradictions to intensify thematic points in this savage and darkly poetic tale. Ultimately, though, under all the shaved heads and swastika-tattooed flesh, *In the Light of You* is a story of redemption and the hope that it's never too late to change: a person, a group, a community, or a civilization."

—*Chicago Tribune*

"I used to think *American History X* was hardcore, that it pushed the envelope and was a really brave story about what hatred can do to you. Then I read Nathan Singer's masterpiece *In the Light of You*. Now *American History X* is like a Disney flick to me."

—*Crime Fiction Dossier*

"A brutal, unflinching look at America's racist subculture, replete with sex, violence, and jagged-edged punk rock. Nathan Singer does more than narrate the story of the rootless, disaffected kids drawn into the hate; he lets you hear the siren song that lures them to their doom."

—J.D. Rhoades, author of *The Devil's Right Hand*

Also available from Nathan Singer and Gallery Books

A Prayer for Dawn
Chasing the Wolf

IN THE
LIGHT
OF YOU

NATHAN SINGER

Gallery Books

New York   London   Toronto   Sydney   New Delhi

G

Gallery Books
An Imprint of Simon & Schuster, Inc.
1230 Avenue of the Americas
New York, NY 10020

This Gallery Books trade paperback edition August 2021

GALLERY BOOKS and colophon are registered trademarks
of Simon & Schuster, Inc.

For information about special discounts for bulk purchases,
please contact Simon & Schuster Special Sales at 1-866-506-1949 or
business@simonandschuster.com.

The Simon & Schuster Speakers Bureau can bring authors to
your live event. For more information or to book an event,
contact the Simon & Schuster Speakers Bureau at 1-866-248-3049 or
visit our website at www.simonspeakers.com.

Interior design by Lana J. Roff

Manufactured in the United States of America

10 9 8 7 6 5 4 3 2 1

Library of Congress Cataloging-in-Publication Data is available.

ISBN 978-1-9821-7492-7
ISBN 978-1-4405-3225-2 (ebook)

PREFACE

AS I WRITE THIS, I am packaging up some of my early works to be archived at the Cincinnati Art Museum. Among the collection is a hardcover first edition of *In the Light of You*. It's an honor to be sure, but as I sit here, I cannot help but wish that this novel truly was nothing more than a museum piece. I wish I could look at this book, chuckle, and say, "Man, was I off base!" I wish this novel, with its angry, gun-toting young white men waging violent terror in the streets, was a relic of a bygone era. I wish everyone who had suggested I was being overly lurid and sensationalistic in my depictions of these racist youth gangs, and paranoid when I claimed they would only grow in power and influence as the twenty-first century progressed, had been correct. I wish I were eating crow right now.

Perhaps when I had the character Richard Lovecraft (de facto leader of the "Fifth Reich" Skins) announce to his gang that "we have friends in important places" and "we will succeed" in America where the German Third Reich had failed, I was being too moderate in vision. I certainly hadn't predicted the risable clowns of the "alt-right," as we now call it. If I had, *In the Light of You* would have needed to be cataloged as a broad Swiftian satire in 2008 rather than a bildungsroman.

To understand where the movement was in the mid-1990s, when the bulk of *In the Light of You* takes place, it makes some sense to start with the only book many of its participants had ever read, *The Turner Diaries*. After serving as an aide to George Lincoln Rockwell of the American Nazi Party in the 1960s, Dr. William Pierce took over the National Youth Alliance (later shortened to National Alliance) as a means of attracting younger people to the white-supremacist movement, and in 1978 he wrote and published *The Turner Diaries* under the name Andrew Macdonald.

For readers not familiar with extreme-right movements, there is often some confusion as to how a novel like *The Turner Diaries*—with its ludicrous plot; drab, virtually nonexistent dialogue; and monotonous, one-dimensional narrator—could have such a profound impact on its readership. Indeed, that novel has directly influenced several high-profile acts of violence and terror: robberies, arson, counterfeiting, murder (most notoriously the 1998 dragging death of African American man James Byrd Jr.), and, of course, Timothy McVeigh's 1995 bombing of the Murrah Building in Oklahoma City. I would hold, however, that the book is best examined not as a work of fiction (though it ostensibly is) but for what it was always meant to be: a recruitment tool for the white power movement. As a narrative it may be a flop, but as an exercise in propaganda and persuasion, there is no doubt it has proven dangerously effective.

Pierce was a hateful man with a loathsome agenda, but he was hardly a fool. He knew full well that including character depth and complexity would be counterproductive to his intentions. As a narrator, Earl Turner has no real voice of his own. He only regurgitates the party lines. He has no feelings of self-doubt, insecurity, or even remorse, and because Turner never experiences doubt or failure, he is the perfect avatar for how Pierce wanted these angry young white men (who are riddled with fears and anxieties about their own weaknesses, self-worth, and perceived powerlessness) to see themselves and, by extension, the movement. It is exactly this lack of humanity that causes Turner to look like a soulless monster to those of us outside the movement, and makes him so appealing to the target audience, who are drawn to monsters because monsters are powerful, fearless, and simple.

I would like to think of *In the Light of You* as the "anti–*Turner Diaries*": a story that is actually about human beings, flawed, complicated, and repellant though they may be; the antithesis of dogma and propaganda; a story that explores a range of human emotions, not just blind hate. *Hate is boring*. Evil is boring. For that matter, the dichotomy of "good vs. evil" is rather dull and tedious. I prefer to explore the hazier, shadowy places of the human experience. Is *In the Light of You* about the "dangers of hate"? I suppose, in part, though that feels reductive.

I'd like to think that all of the racial, sexual, and sociopolitical elements could be excised from this novel and the center of the narrative would still hold; that at its core it's really about a confused young guy (and an equally confused young lady) just trying to "figure it all out" and screwing up pretty badly in the process. If *In the Light of You* is about the "danger" of anything, it's about the danger of unquestioned obedience to an ideology, particularly if it is delivered by a charismatic figurehead—a *great, shining light*.

Beware the lights.

They may bring warmth and illumination.

They may bring blindness, and fire.

Nathan Singer
2020

ONE

It's hard to know how to feel when your best friend blows out a man's stomach with a shotgun. Self-defense, you understand. The guy had a knife. Picture it: my friend is sitting in his trailer one evening making moves on his lady du jour, when there comes a banging on the window. The girl's ex stumbles in drunk waving a butterfly knife, screaming, "Bitch! You broke my heart! Can't you see I love you, you fucking cunt!?!" because he's a smooth operator, see, with lyrics to spare. My friend says, "Get the fuck out!" Guy goes to stab, triggers are pulled, messes are made. Hands are cuffed. Courts are adjourned. Not guilty. Like I said, it's hard to know how to feel.

"Congratulations."

"I had to," he said.

"I understand completely."

"It was him or me, Mikey."

"No doubt."

"I'm eighteen this month. I coulda gotten death."

"Dodged that bullet."

"It's not like I'm not sorry it happened."

"Hey man, I'm here for you."

But I wasn't. We moved away from Louisville not long

after that. Not because my friend decorated a double-wide with a dude's intestines. Dad just thought there'd be better work in Ohio. He was right . . . more or less. This was 1994. I was fourteen. It was nearly three years before I had another friend. That's just the way it is.

PEOPLE OFTEN ASK ME, "What was it that made you decide to dedicate your life to hate?" They want an answer that starts with, "Well, you see, I was hurt this one time . . ." And when people ask me, "What was it that turned you around?" they want an answer like, "Jesus." Or, "Jail really opened my eyes." Or, "Soandso taught me the meaning of love / peace / tolerance / *inserthippieshitbuzzwordhere*." But none of that is right. My answer to both is, "Nothing."

MY DAD IS A boiler operator. Or rather, he was until the accident. Mom is a telemarketer. At least fifty times on an average day my mother is invited to go fuck herself, get cancer, die a fiery death, or suck any number of anatomical bits and pieces. If she works after 9:00 PM she gets an extra two dollars an hour. Good times.

Let's get one thing straight: my parents are not stupid people. But it's safe to say that academia was never in their cards. I mean, my name is Mikal. M-I-K-A-L. Because the "chae" in "Michael" made them nervous. When we moved up north a piece in 1994 they were both thirty years old. You do the math.

I'm glad the plan to move to Ohio did not include hopes of leaving the manslaughter behind, because that would've been mighty disappointing. Finances being what they were, we ended up in a little pocket of the world called Blackchurch. Although that name is shorthand for the whole eastern side of the neighborhood, the area that can rightfully be called

Blackchurch is really just one intersection where Blackstone Street crosses Desmond Road (or even just one of the four actual churches that occupy the adjacent corners). And you see, a million years before Christ was born Desmond Road was called Churchwalk, and everyone in the neighborhood still calls it that. Get that wrong and you expose yourself as a Blackchurch virgin. Not a good thing to be. Another thing not to be in Blackchurch is white.

YOU GO TO SLEEP there every night to the sound of gunfire. To this day I toss and turn in fits of restless slumber without the melodious sounds of the *ratta-tat-tat bop pop tagow*. We hadn't been there but two months when I watched a boy get shot in the face at midday. I'm out by the basketball courts by the old, abandoned YMCA building, delusional enough to think that I might get in on a game, when this young homeboy makes the scene, pulls a 9mm out of his shorts, and blasts this other young cat right in the forehead. I duck behind a big yellow LTD. Folks are screaming, running for cover. And glacier-cool, the boy caps the poor son of a bitch once more in the thigh, walks up to a girl who's curled up on the sidewalk screeching and bawling, and goes, "How ya like me, huh?" And then he just strolls away. (When I think about that now, I hear the funky bassline of his theme song kick in just then. Sort of a Curtis Mayfield / Isaac Hayes kinda joint.) The boy he shot lay on the sidewalk crying, "I need uh amboolass! I NEED UH AMBOOLASS!!!" the blood from his temple spilling into his mouth, spraying out with every wail.

Sirens sang in the distance, advancing. Paramedics pulled up, tossed him on a stretcher, slapped a mask on him. They peeled his shorts off the bullet wound with *shhhhhhhlt*, his thigh shredded and burnt like barbecue gone wrong. I didn't see the exit wound, but it was enough to make one of the paramedics gasp, "Motheragod on a pogo stick!" So they loaded the boy into the wagon, rolled away, and that was that. That was that. I never heard what happened to him.

I sat on the curb, leaning against the LTD, locked up so tight you could bounce a quarter off of me. This baller from the court came walking over, shirtless and sweaty, hair half-fro'd / half cornrowed.

"How 'boutcha, whiteboy?"

"How about me what?"

"Welcome to Niggatown," he said, and headed on back to his game. He hadn't really even looked at me. His name was D'antre Philips. And I would grow to hate him.

BLACKCHURCH IS FIFTEEN MINUTES from downtown proper as the Metro rolls. Twenty to University Village, but it may as well be a million. Blackchurch is an island. It is its own nation with its own language and law. The rule for non-blacks around those parts was simple: act black or suffer. And the Catch-22 addendum to the first part of the rule is "quit tryin' ta perp." If you wanted to at least attempt to play their game, the uniform was set and not to be altered: XXL white T-shirt / XXXL blue jeans. It is to date the most startling example of voluntary conformity in all of recorded history, and I should know. Don't get me wrong, I understood the concept behind it perfectly. Like many young men I always dreamed of being a soldier. The idea of being part of a perfectly oiled, perfectly regimented fighting machine . . . *damn* . . . that's pure power. A wall of strength. One mind. Charge in, search and destroy. So boys make armies in the streets. But I knew I'd never make rank there.

D'antre Philips was one of the many low-rent thugs to populate our little hamlet. He sold a bit of dope, drove a car far out of his price range, played "da hoes" like it was his job, and spent his money on big, ugly gold jewelry as he continued to live off his mother well into his twenties. As he was a little older, he acted as the de facto leader of a small group of local players: Arnold Lincoln, Arnold's older brother Tremaine, Ezekial Johnson, Rakeem Hollis, the Willis twins, and token white nigger Jack Curry. Of all the people in the neighborhood for whom I had no love, I hated Jack Curry most of all. I'm not going to tap-dance around the fact: I was terrified of him. A lot of people were. "There go that crazy white muh-fucka Jack," folks would say, "so jus' keep yo' distance." And believe me, the fear was justified. I know that better than most. Myriad rumors about him echoed in hushed tones throughout the neighborhood, and after what I've seen I have no reason to doubt a single one of them.

At first it seemed Jack Curry rolled with D'antre Philips and that crowd completely on his own terms. He gained respect by bringing every ass-thumping he received back on his attackers tenfold. He didn't wear the uniform. He didn't play the game. In fact, he didn't look like anything else in town. He wore his hair down to his belt, knotted into dread-locks that he dyed black and oxblood red. He wore shirts by bands like EYEHATEGOD that read "Kill Your Boss." He was coated in tattoos like something out of a nineteenth-century circus sideshow. (I'm fond of tattoos myself and have a number of them, as do most of the people I know. But that fucker was more colored paint than man.)

This is the only conversation I ever had with Jack Curry: "Hey dude," I said. "Your ink work is badass."

"Just trying to cover the white up," he growled, and kept walking. Never even looked me in the eye.

Just trying to cover the white up. That was why I detested him. His seething, undying contempt for white people made me shudder. Curry grew up right there on Blackstone Street, and his response to a childhood spent abused for his skin color was to hate *us*, his own kind. I wasn't particularly up on racial ideology at that time, but it seemed to me even then that self-loathing of that magnitude could only lead to horrible things. I definitely hold to that belief today.

FROM 1994 TO 1996 I kept completely to myself. I had no friends. I didn't speak to one single girl. Either at school or at "home" I dealt with no one I wasn't forced to. I was beaten, threatened, robbed, ridiculed, and run down as a matter of habit. By the time my dad had destroyed his hand on the job and his drinking had gotten so out of control that he had to be taken away, there wasn't an eight-by-eight stretch of this earth where I felt all right. I was an alien in every space. I couldn't even wrap myself in some fake nostalgia for my own friends in Louisville. I just didn't feel it.

THE ONE SLICE OF joy I had during that period came as a bit of schadenfreude when D'antre Philips's little gang disintegrated. In the tireless pursuit of absolute insufferability it seems the well of ideas had all but run dry, and some time in '95 D'antre Philips discovered politics. Needless to say, shortly thereafter the rest of them did likewise. Philips, reinventing himself as a boho MC called Daddy Molotov, started some "conscious" rap group and began seriously pursuing the craft of writing—which did exactly nothing to keep him out of prison. (Life being the baffling mess that it is, he recently published a book for children, which he wrote in jail. It's called *Princess Africa Jones*. There's just no telling.) Arnold Lincoln, taking "black awareness" to new heights, changed his name to Senbe Shabazz and cut all ties to white people . . . Jack Curry in particular. The two had a frighteningly heated public falling-out where the police had to be called and property was damaged (little did I know then, but I would come to play a part in reuniting these two men . . . a role about which I'm conflicted, to say the least). Jack Curry, in some capacity, took up with Ezekial Johnson's sister Lisa, who by that time had changed her name to Niani Shange (nee-AH-nee SHON-gay). They enrolled in university and—strap yourself in because it's just so shocking—became lefty cause-heads. I doubt they realized at the time what an explosive decision that would turn out to be.

NONE OF THIS MEANT much of anything to me at the time. I was busy struggling through high school where, thanks to God and his cruel sense of humor, I was once again one of few whites. I wore my hair in a crew cut at that time and was decked out in camo every day, taking the whole "army of one" concept to heart. I had big plans to enroll in the Air Force. On the rare occasion that I actually showed up for school I was attacked and tormented without fail. That's just the way it was.

I WAS A SOPHOMORE, sixteen, one quarter from expulsion, when I met Joe and Phil. They were both eighteen and had been shuffled through pretty much every public school in the system. This was their last chance at state-enforced education. I'd seen them once before about a week prior, likely when they first arrived, but didn't think much of it at the time.

I was sitting in third bell, Algebra I, and these two girls behind me were having a bit of fun at my expense: ruminating at length about the size and quality of my dick, which, by their estimation, probably didn't amount to much. *Where's the fucking teacher?* I thought, trying to ignore them, torching up inside, but keeping still and quiet on the surface. I'd been down this road plenty, and I never seemed to know the right way to turn. Finally,

"Psssssst! White boy! Yo, white boy!"

And it just came out . . .

"What the hell do you want, black girl?"

Fuck.

"OOOOOoooooh, no no no no no no no no no no no no NO! NO you di'en't! You did NOT jus' call me 'blackgirl.' Uh uh."

People started to laugh and taunt me. I'm catching erasers to the head and all sorts of slurs about my family tree and the color of my neck (which had to have been mighty red by that point).

"You called me 'whiteboy,'" I said, trying to remain cool. "I called you 'blackgirl.' Adds up real nice the way I see it. Stop me if I'm going too fast for you."

"Fool! You betta rekuhnize!"

"I recognize that you ain't got much manners." I continued digging my own grave. "Didn't your mother and father teach you nothing? But then, you probably ain't got a father, do you?"

"Awwwwwwwwwwwwwwww SHIT!"

"Did you just insult this here fine sista, punk?" some homeboy said, getting right in my face. "I know you wouldn't dare use 'at tone with a BLACK woman. Original woman. Mother of da Earf."

"He sho NUFF did! Fuck 'im up!"

This is how I figured I would die, I thought to myself . . . when out of the blue one of the new transfers, silent to this point, decided to chime in.

"Just punch the fucking chimp, kid," he said to me. "Just jack him in the mouth. Look at them gi-normous lips. It won't even hurt your fist." We all turned around to see this thick, shaven-headed Caucasian side of beef, smiling like a sunny afternoon. Phil Reider by name. Seated next to him was a fellow named Joe Briggan. They were dressed in identical gear down to the white laces in their black books: bowling jackets, red suspenders, neck tats that each read "white power." They both leaned in with a cocksure arrogance that I had never seen on white people. Ever.

"You just say somethin' to me, peckawood?" the homeboy asked, hissing, his cheek twitching furiously as everyone braced for the inevitable.

"No, Rochester, I didn't," Phil answered casually. "I said something about you. When you hear the words, 'Go fetch my slippers, Darkie,' THEN you'll know I'm talking to you."

And then, the mayhem.

The entire class spilled out into the hallway on a wave of flying fists. Unbeknownst to anyone, Phil and Joe were packing an arsenal's worth of weapons: blackjacks, chains, brass knuckles, which almost, but not quite, leveled the playing field. I got in my licks and took a few as well, but strangely enough, I wasn't really all that scared. One of my brand-new lifelong friends handed me a retracting baton, which I flipped to its full extension and swung as widely as my arm would reach. Aiming for legs, I built a comfortable little force field all about me. It took a good half of the faculty plus all of the assistant football coaches to subdue the melee and separate the offending parties. We were all expelled. Surprise.

MY PARENTS DIDN'T CARE that I was no longer in school. And even if they had it wouldn't have made any difference to me, for I saw very little of them after that. I've seen very little of them since.

Phil and Joe took me to meet their crew.

"This here's Mikal Fanon, y'all. He's a bad mamma jamma and he don't take no guff."

Phil and Joe were the youngest of the group. At least of the guys. The rest were all in their early- to midtwenties. Top dog was a fellow named Richard Lovecraft.

Richard's got a way about him, everyone would say. *That Richard's just got a special something.*

"Welcome to the revolution, Mike," Richard said, shaking my hand and chucking my shoulder as if he'd been patiently awaiting my arrival, and now that I was here all could rock 'n' roll as scheduled. Within minutes of meeting this guy I couldn't help but notice how he could dictate the mood of the room with a look or a joke or the tone of his voice. (In all the time I would spend with Richard from that day on I'd see him work that same energy over and over again, with groups as small as two or crowds of hundreds, and always with the same ease.) You could have told me he was a rock star or the middleweight champion or the Prime fucking Minister and I wouldn't have batted an eye or thought it at all dubious. And if you had told me right at that moment, *You will follow that man off the edge of the earth*, I would have told you to go fuck yourself . . . but you'd have been right.

"You proud to be white, kid?" somebody asked me.

"Oh, yeah, sure," I stuttered. "I mean not so much proud as grateful, you know?"

Silence. Not even so much as a shrug. Feeling the need to qualify, I continued, "I mean, my mom, you know, got it on with my dad. He's white, she's white, here I am reflecting sunlight. Worked out well. Should pay off at job interviews and shit. So big thanks to Mom for her discriminating tastes. Coulda gone some other way maybe. I guess ole Mom coulda fucked a Samoan, or one of them Ugandan tribesmen who wear dinner plates as lip jewelry. But she didn't. I think that showed real class."

Seven and a half miles away an old woman dropped a thimble on her kitchen floor. I know that because I heard it plain as day. Then, all at once, everyone fell about the place roaring with laughter. Richard most of all.

"That," Richard said, wiping a tear from his eye, "is the single best answer I've ever heard. I hope you people are taking notes. Somebody get this boy a beer." And somebody did.

TWO

From that day forth Richard's pad became my hangout. I never officially "joined" the Fifth Reich in any ceremonial way. There was no initiation, no memorizing philosophies or swearing allegiance to anything. We just all hung out there drinking brew, talking about chicks, listening to tunes, playing cards. Before too long I started crashing there. Not long after that I pretty much became Richard's roommate.

Late at night after everyone else had left or cashed out, Richard and I would stay up shooting the shit until sunrise. Not about anything specific, just whatever came to mind. He gave me books to read, mostly detective thrillers and true-crime stories, occasionally historical nonfiction. He'd warn me ahead of time what was a fun read and what was "a little dry," and said it was up to me if I wanted to read the shit or not. I devoured everything he gave me.

It was all badass and brand-new . . . but it all felt familiar as well. Lived-in. It felt *right* to me.

I REMEMBER MY FIRST warehouse rally like it's the only memory worth having. I remember the fear and the anticipation as we drove for what seemed like hours through cracked-out ghettoes, farms and fields, and miles upon miles of industrial wasteland. I remember the mob of bald heads and liberty spikes filing into the most bombed-out-looking structure I had ever seen.

The stage was set with amps and a drum kit. Behind it hung a banner, which read, "The Hangmen." The walls were lined with kegs every which way. The smell of impending ruckus hung in the air in rippling sheets. There weren't a lot of girls there that night, but the ones who were present were all gorgeous: blondes and goths and fine pixie punk babies. Some older roughneck was on stage screaming about "taking out the trash," but people were cheering and "sieg heiling" so loudly I could barely make it out. I wasn't really interested anyway because I had designs on a little punk rock girl named Suzi who had driven with us and was friends with Joe's and Phil's current squeezes, Anne and Reeba. (I've heard other Skins lament the overall lack of women in the movement, but I can honestly say that in Richard's gang we never wanted for tail. Call it luck.) Suzi was sixteen like me, and had only been with the Fifth Reich for a couple of weeks. I grabbed us both a beer and we tried to find a place where we could talk, which was pretty much impossible. Over the cacophony I picked up that Suzi had a fairly rotten home life. Her mother beat her and tormented her. She had a bandage on her brow over her left eye that night because her mother had smacked her in the face with a broom handle. Her eye was bruised maroon, with just a shade of emerald. She loved her father, though, and hoped that he would divorce her mother and she could go off to live with him. I was as interested as I needed to be.

I was just about to ask her if she'd like to step outside for a bit of air when we heard the roughneck holler, ". . . And it's my pleasure to invite to this stage . . . y'all know you love him . . . RICHARD FUCKING LOVECRAFT!!!"

The roar of the crowd was so intense just then that you

would have thought Sid Vicious had risen from the grave and walked through the door. Suzi and I wedged up as close to the stage as we could. I knew he was cool, but I hadn't realized until right then just how important Richard was to the movement. He was *the star*. The bright shining light.

"So hot . . . ," Suzi whispered to herself as she watched Richard take to the mic. To look at the rest of the women in the crowd, the sentiment was universal.

"I'm not going to waste your time with a lot of blah blah blah, cuz we all know who we're really here for . . . ," Richard said, and everyone cheered, throwing up their hands in salute. From there he talked about taking the country back from the mud people and sending the liberals back to Woodstock, and it was all very funny and sharp. But truth be told, he could have stood there and read from *Goodnight Moon* and he would have still had those people in the palm of his tattooed hand. *Richard's got a special something about him. Richard's just got a way.*

". . . So are you just about ready?!" Richard yelled. The crowd cheered. "What, are you fuckers asleep out there?!?! I said ARE YOU FUCKING READY TO GO FUCKING BATSHIT?!?!?!"

ROOOOOOOOOOOOOOOOOOOOOOOOOOOOO-OOOAAAAAAAARRRRR!!!!!

"Then bash your fucking skulls together for THE HANG-MEN!!!"

The crowd erupted, and Richard dove in, riding the wave of hands all the way to the back wall of the warehouse. Four gruesome-looking mutants who looked like they just crawled out of a sewer somewhere took to the stage, grabbed their instruments and let loose with a ferocious, "WHITE POWW-WWWWEEEER!"

Four chords, four beats per measure, and a cluster bomb of unbridled rage:

One two three four

We want our Racial Holy War!
Five six seven eight
Let the monkeys feel our hate!
Nine ten eleven twelve
Send the faggots straight to Hell!
Here it is the final hour
Dirty Jew, time for your shower!
RAHOWA!!!!!!!!!

Bodies collided with bodies. People dove from the window ledges down into the swarming mass. Blistering hardcore bludgeoned us back from the stage and we charged back in screaming for more. And everyone knew the words:

One two three four
This is how we settle the score!
Five six seven eight
The White Man reigns, it is our fate!
Nine ten eleven twelve
Every mud fuck for himself!
The time has come for true White Power
C'mon, Jew, it's just a shower!
RAHOWA!!!!!!!!!!!!!!

I didn't know the lyrics yet, but I was damn sure I'd know them all word for word before next time. As Suzi pogo'd in place I hurled myself into the throng. Tearing off my shirt I let my skinny arms flail. *I am a tornado.* RAHOWA!!!!!!! *What does it mean?* RAHOWA!!!!!!! *I'll figure it out.* RA-HOWA!!!!!!!!!! *It's the only thing that matters to me now.* RA-HOWA!!!!!! I screamed it at the top of my lungs.

We slammed and skanked and punched and drank and bled away the hours. Every song just like the one before it, yet somehow better. Pride. Strength. Unified. Power. *An army.*

THE DRIVE BACK HOME seemed to take no time at all. The van was packed to its splitting point, as we appeared to have twice the crew we had on the ride there. Suzi and I rode in the far back—the perfect place to be.

"Yup yup," she said. "I'm so happy right now."

"How come?"

"Because you have your arm around me."

And I did and I didn't even realize. We stayed that way the whole ride.

Everyone else was asleep except for Richard, who drove, and a girl Richard had picked up at the rally. I don't remember her name. We all called her Special Olympics. Special Olympics was Barbie-doll hot, but nowhere near as smart. This girl had it all: tight acid-washed jeans, white high-top tennis shoes, hot pink halter top, fried blonde Jersey-girl coral reef hair. The whole package. I mention her only because she hung around for about a month and a half. Richard grew weary of her after a couple of days and passed her along to Brian. At one point she and Brian had a tiff and he threw her out of the house completely bare-ass naked. Somehow, without any money or a stitch of clothing on, she made it back to Kentucky. She was only mad at him for a day or so. Last I heard she's a hairstylist at some high-end boutique and she strips on the weekends. And she's pregnant by some Mexican with a tattoo of Jesus on his cheek. The most memorable thing about Special Olympics was that you could hear her having an orgasm from out in the driveway. Like guinea pigs in a blender.

We made it home from the rally at about 3:00 AM. Richard's apartment was actually half of a house, just southeast of downtown, right outside the Metroline. No one occupied the other half of the building so we pretty much infiltrated that as well. People grabbed space to crash wherever they could. Suzi and I staked out prime real estate on the screened-in back porch. I dragged a couple of sleeping bags out from the closet and pulled some cushions off of a beat-up old sofa. Suzi stripped down to her panties. I peeled off my sweat-soaked jeans and lay next to her. She ran her fingers over my neck, my face, and through my short, bristly hair.

"So what's the style here exactly," she asked, "crew cut or fade?"

"Huh?"

"I mean," she giggled, "are you tryin' to look like a jarhead or a nigger?"

"Well, I ain't trying to look like no nigger."

"Okay, that's a start."

Not the most romantic repartee you're likely to hear, *but fuck it*. After we ran out of dumb shit to talk about we got rest-of-the-way naked and down to business. Still pumped up from the rally, I thought I did pretty well and was mighty pleased with myself. But afterward Suzi patted me on the back and said, "That's okay. It happens sometimes. No need to be embarrassed." That's just the way it is.

SUZI FELL ASLEEP SHORTLY thereafter, but I was wide-awake. I yanked my jeans back on and went into the house to scrounge up some vittles. I found Richard in the kitchen rummaging through the fridge, and finding naught but a sack of geriatric french fries and what was hopefully a kiwi. Boots and boxer shorts was all he wore, his multitude of tattoos glistening with perspiration. Clearly he and Special Olympics had had a far more vigorous workout than Suzi and me.

"Some night, eh Mikey?"

"You're telling me."

"I just want to say, I'm really glad you're with us, man. I can tell you're a thinker. It's good to have another thinking man around."

"Cool. Thanks."

"You do drugs?"

"Nope."

"Not even weed?"

"No way."

"Good. Glad to hear it. Fuck that hippie shit. I don't allow it in my house. Makes your mind slow." He cracked two cans of Foster's and handed one to me. We toasted. I hadn't realized it, but I was humming that Hangmen song. "One, two, three, four . . ."

"You like that tune?" Richard asked.

"Shit yeah. It rocks like holy hell."

"You wanna learn how to play it?"

"I can't play guitar."

"Dude, it's punk rock. Anybody can play it."

Richard went and fetched a beat-up old Larrivée. He handed it to me and wrapped his hand around mine to show me the fingering.

"Now see this? This is a G power chord. Three fingers: the root note, the fifth, and the octave. You use this same shape for all the chords up and down the neck. Give it a shot."

I gave it a shot. It sounded like hog balls. Richard laughed and ruffled my hair.

"Keep practicing. You'll get it."

So I did. And he was right. If any of you were wondering how to play "Count Them Off" by The Hangmen, it goes like this:

THE HANGMEN—COUNT THEM OFF

G
ONE TWO THREE FOUR
C　　　　　　　**D**
WE WANT OUR RACIAL / HOLY WAR!
G
FIVE SIX SEVEN EIGHT
C　　　　　　　**D**
LET THE MONKEYS / FEEL OUR HATE!
G
NINE TEN ELEVEN TWELVE
C　　　　　　　**D**
SEND THE FAGGOTS / STRAIGHT TO HELL!
G
HERE IT IS THE FINAL HOUR
C　　　　　　　**D**
DIRTY JEW, TIME / FOR YOUR SHOWER!
E
RAHOWA!!!!!!!!!
C
RAHOWA!!!!!!!!!
E
RAHOWA!!!!!!!!! OI!
C　　　　　　**G**
RAHOWAAAAAAAAAAAAAAAAAA!!!!!!!!!

"SO, MIKE. TELL ME. You have an issue. One that really matters to you. What is it?"

"I ain't political, Rich. I don't have no issues really."

"You're not in high school now," he said, looking me straight in the eyes. "It's just you and me talking in the kitchen at four thirty in the morning with no shirts on. I hear those wheels in your head turning from out here. Tell me what's going on in there."

"Well . . . ," I said, and it dawned on me that what I was about to tell him I had never told anyone before, "I'm kind of concerned about, you know, things about the environment and whatnot." I expected him to scoff and roll his eyes, but he just nodded. I had his full attention. So I continued, "You know, like global warming and pollution and all."

"Go on," he said.

"My family is, well, I guess, kind of poor."

"Yeah."

"And we've lived in lots of different low-income areas, like by the river, okay. In the fucking floodplain of course. And it seems to me that big corporations get away with dumping their waste near poor neighborhoods and in creeks that run by more . . . impoverished areas, you know, and I'm thinking that's fucked up. I mean, no wonder so many people, kids and all, in like West Virginia and shit, are sick. Right? I don't know. I guess I sound like some fucking, whooooo! Peace and love queer-ass right now."

"Hell no you don't," Richard said emphatically, then looking around to see if he had awakened anyone. "You are absolutely right, Mike. Absolutely. Our planet is being ravaged by poison and people don't give a rat's ass about it. You think that fat fuck Clinton or his bosses care? Yeah, sure. But . . . you know who was actively working for the environment way back before the tie-dyes hugged their first tree? *Hitler*."

"Zat right?"

"Hitler. The great bogeyman of history. The Third Reich

were promoting and enacting ecological initiatives since day one."

"I didn't know that."

"How could you? You're not gonna learn it in the public schools, that's for damn sure. It doesn't fit within the framework of their propaganda. If it doesn't conform to the dogma of multiculturalism, then snip, snip, out it goes. The truth just doesn't suit their agenda. And that's why we have to fight."

I DIDN'T KNOW WHAT to think. I didn't want to think right then. Not about ecology or school or the president or world history or any of it. I just wanted in. I wanted boots and white laces. I wanted red braces for my pants. I wanted my uniform. I wanted in the army. This army.

Richard must have sensed it, and he crooked his finger and headed off down the hall. I followed him. There I stood in the doorway of the bathroom looking at myself in the full-length mirror.

"You mentioned your family," he said, rummaging around in a small cabinet filled with odds and ends. "Are you close with them?" I shrugged. "You have any brothers or sisters?" I didn't answer, for I was busy mapping out where all my tattoos would go. An eagle on my left shoulder. A swastika over my heart. "RAHOWA" across my stomach. And, of course, "white power" on my neck. White power. *WHITE POWER.* White man. *I'm a WHITE man.* White Power.

"Well, it doesn't matter," he said. "You've got brothers now. A shit ton of them."

Without another word Richard clicked on his electric razor and ran it across my scalp. My hair sprinkled down to my shoulders and across the bathroom tiles. I watched in the mirror and saw the person I used to be, whomever he was, disappearing. Then gone. *Goodbye and good riddance to me.*

THREE

I'm often asked how True Aryan Warriors spend their time day in and day out. Let me tell you, there is a lot of *Tetris* involved. And the importance of *Sonic the Hedgehog* to the struggle for total ethnic supremacy simply cannot be overstated. Speaking just for my chapter, we also spent an inordinate number of afternoons at vinyl record swap meets, Richard being the most dedicated vinyl fetishist I'd ever met before or since. If I had a halfpence for every time I heard him say, "Ahhh vinyl . . . why listen to anything else?" I could self-publish this book, believe me. My assertion that digital recording was far and away superior to analog fell on deaf ears, to say the very least. ("It fell upon hostile ears" would be an odd thing to say, but not altogether inaccurate.)

That's not to say that we weren't active. There were parties most nights of the week, and a rally at least once a month. And, of course, the fights. Up until the time I joined I had been in my share of scraps and street scuffles. But in the Reich we would have battles like other people had neighborhood get-togethers. Most were planned, few were fair. Even if the rest of us were clueless about the where, when, who, and why of any rumble, Richard knew and he knew just how to win. And if it got hotter than he had thought it would he always knew the way out (well . . . almost always). After SHARPs (Skin Heads Against Racial Prejudice), Richard's favorite targets were military folk. Marines especially. Richard held that marines were nothing but the Government's sheep, and "his army" could take out "theirs" any time. He batted a thousand as far as that went, but I'd be lying if I said that there was anything fair about it. This would usually take place in a bar, most often our favorite haunt Eldon's Tavern, which was run by an old guard racialist whom Richard had known since he was preteen. El was with our cause, so he never gave us static about me or the girls being underage, and he always covered for us when the police were called. It would start when one of us would insult some soldier boy's wench. This was particularly effective if said wench was non-white. Richard would then walk over extending an olive branch, pretending to be the voice of reason, then he would smash the biggest guy over the head with a bottle or a beer mug. We would then swarm the rest of them, their ladies included, with pool sticks, chairs, what have you. That's just the way it was.

Rumbling with SHARPs was even more ludicrous. These showdowns were actually scheduled ahead of time. "We'll meet you on the floor at the Agnostic Front show . . ." Idiocy. SHARPs were so easy to beat because invariably at least a couple of their guys would be racialist undercover. Call it the COINTELPRO of the white underground. The only time that backfired was at the Kreator concert when the lead singer stopped in the middle of the song "Betrayer," pointed us out, and admonished the rest of the crowd to, "Kill zoze fucking racist pigs!" We made a break for it out the back of the venue and escaped unscathed. Everyone else thought it was hilarious, but I was pissed off because I really liked Kreator, and I still do.

Within the group I was seen as something of an "intellectual." There's just no telling. I suppose because I actually read the books Richard recommended. Although I was the youngest, there was a sense that at least some of the guys deferred to me. Some even jokingly referred to me as the Minister of Information. (That's indeed a joke because we did not have ranks. Technically Richard was not even "the leader" in any official way. But he was. And everybody knew it. That's just the way it was.) The fact that Richard appeared to value my input and respect my intelligence carried all the weight. Who was I to protest?

I IMAGINE THAT THERE is a moment in everyone's life that is THE moment. *That was the crossroads*, you'll say to yourself, *and if I'd taken a different path everything would have worked out differently.* You only spot it after the fact, of course, and it has to seem innocuous at the time. The biggest of the Big Stuff doesn't hinge on Sophie's Choice, it hides behind, "Hey, what do y'all wanna do tonight?" Maybe other people have more than one THE moment in their lives. Maybe I will too someday. But as for right now I have just the one night. It was my seventeenth birthday.

Everything, I feel, that had happened in my life leading up to that night, as rough as it may have been, had pretty well gone as scheduled. And everything since has followed the course set that night. On the evening of my seventeenth birthday I had no idea that I would be making a flip o' the coin decision that would ultimately mean the difference between life and death. I could have just as easily chosen something else. We could have gone out for burgers. We could have gone to the movies. We could have burned down some old abandoned apartment complex. But that's all *the other.* There is only *what we did* and *the other.* I have no idea where the other path would have led. Maybe to the same place in the end. But I doubt it.

LIKE I SAID, IT was my seventeenth birthday. Richard's pad was packed with crazed hooligans. Final Solution on the stereo, beer was flowing, people were dancing and skanking this way and that. Richard was smart enough to have nothing of value in what passed for the living room, as bedlam and mayhem were the norm around his place. The TV had been stuffed in the closet along with the stereo console. There were a couple of already-broken couches that ended up completely demolished that night, and a recliner that never really had a prayer. Everything worth anything was kept in Richard's bedroom, which no one but he and invited guests could enter. He even took down his beloved Nazi flag that night and rehung it in the bedroom, where it pretty well stayed from then on.

Within our little circle of friends the notion began to float about that we should ditch the party for a while, head out on our own, and come back later ready to rage the night away. We could have stayed right there, of course. We could have gone for a walk or hitchhiked to Detroit. Somebody said, "It's up to the birthday boy." To which I replied, "Sure. Fuck it. Let's head downtown for a drink or two." And that's what we did.

SUZI WAS WITH ME, Reeba with Phil, Anne with Joe, and another couple, Jennie and Geoff, came along. Richard and Brian were as yet unattached to anyone. We ended up at this trendy, collegey place called The Stable. All the little students were scrubbed and squeaky-clean, drinking fruity cocktails, dancing to whatever slug vomit pop radio told them to love that week, and hoping to maybe acquire a little company for the evening. The crowd was a fairly liberal mix of types . . . all in their designated uniforms. And there we were strolling in: six cue-balled knuckleheads in red braces and black bowling jackets wearing four fine and dandy punk rock girls on our arms like it's a grand gala affair. We were not the folks with whom to fuck, the whole club knew it, and good on them for the sharp eye. But although we were in enemy territory that night, we were there on a mission of peace. More or less.

"HEY MIKEY," RICHARD WHISPERED, "what do you think. Worth my time?"

He indicated toward the bar at these two pitiful little skirts sitting overwhelmed and unsure. Neither looked old enough to be there, even to my seventeen-year-old eyes. I wasn't sure which had caught Richard's attention: the knobby-kneed four-eyes who looked like Peppermint Patty's girl toy in the *Peanuts* cartoon, or the wispy little puff of nothing next to her. No sooner did I see them when a raver-boy in outlandishly large blue jeans came up to "Marcie" and whisked her away to the dance floor.

"Which one, Rich, the geek or the leftover?"

"The fucking 'leftover,' jackass," he said, irritated. "She's the one I meant from the get-go."

"She's all right. Go for it."

"Meh . . . we'll see."

Joe ordered us each a pint and we muscled a group of trust-fundies away from the table we decided was ours. The tragic comedy surrounding us on all sides was almost too much to bear. Big Pants and Nerd Girl on the dance floor alone, slobbering on each other like two spastics sharing a mutual fit, was enough to make you bust a gut either laughing or puking.

"Fags over there," Brian said pointing. "Dykes over there. Mutts of every stripe, shade, and stench. Somebody just say the word, I'm ready to stomp this trash."

"Richard," Reeba said, "that baby blonde at the bar is staring at you."

Well, of course she was. Most of the chicks there had their eyes on Richard, even the dark-skinned ones who should know better. Richard looked over at her, raised his glass and smiled. She smiled back all bashful-like and looked intently at her parasol.

"No stomping tonight, Bri," Richard said. "Just sit back and enjoy the freak show."

"Hippie," Phil razzed.

"Yo' mama a hippie, nigga," Richard said jutting out his lips. We laughed and laughed.

AN HOUR AND A half went by, maybe more, and the novelty pretty well wore thin and then out. We did tool with a few chumps stupid enough to get near us, but for the most part playing nice was the rule. Geoff and I headed off to the men's room for a leak. We each took a urinal on either side of a young Middle Eastern gentleman.

"Hey Mike, I think I just pissed on my hand. Could you throw me a towel?"

"Can't help you, Geoff. Maybe Habib here can lean his head over and be a pal."

"My name's not Habib," the fellow sighed. "I'm a Sikh."

"Allah al habbala? Sim salla bim?"

"I don't want any trouble, guys," said Not Habib, zipping up quickly and heading for the door.

"Vell tang you veddy mush!" Geoff called after him. Good times.

As we exited the restroom we spotted the lonely girl at the bar lighting matches and watching them go out in an ashtray. She smiled as her dweebette friend and the skate brat finally made their way back over to her. It didn't last long.

"Hey, uh, Sharon," I heard Nerd Girl say, "how's it going? Listen, I need a big fave."

Poor Lil Thing's eyes were wide with disbelief as her apparent friend told her she needed their dorm room for the evening. Exclusively. "You understand, right? Pay ya back. Promise." And with nary another word spoken, "Marcie" and her fine catch of the evening skipped jauntily away into the night. As tears filled the bright blue eyes of that abandoned and forlorn young maiden, as she stood at the bar lost and alone muttering impotent protests to no one at all, Geoff and I literally fell backward against the wall in peals of laughter.

But then . . . as he is wont to do . . . Superman swooped in and assed up our fun.

"EXCUSE ME?" RICHARD SAID to her, leaning in across the bar. The girl peered up at him with a look that instantly brought gooseflesh up on my back. It was a look close to awe, as if she had known of him already from myth or legend or TV and she couldn't believe that he was really there. Couldn't believe that he was talking to her. I clenched up when I saw it. Like I shouldn't have been there to see it. It wasn't for my eyes, and I was an intruder. It was a look that I knew no woman would ever give me (and, to date, none have). I stopped laughing instantly and felt like a cretin for having done so in the first place. Geoff simply shrugged and headed back to the table. Clearly he did not have the same reaction. I stayed, against the wall, in the shadows.

"I'm sorry to bother you," Richard continued, "but my constituents and I were feeling a bit lonely over there in the corner. We were wondering if you'd like to come join us." He pointed to everyone at the table. They all waved. She giggled and nodded.

"Richard Lovecraft," he said.

"Pleased to meet you," she replied. "Sherry Nicolas."

"Truly my pleasure." A line only Richard could pull off.

I WALKED BACK TO the table a couple of steps behind them. Richard waved me up quickly.

"Sherry, this is my best friend, Mikal Fanon."

"Nice to meet you, Mikal," Sherry said. I smiled weakly and nodded. I was, as they say, thrown for a loop. *Best friend? Did Richard Lovecraft just call me his best friend?*

"It's Mikal's birthday today. He's forty-three."

"Well happy birthday, Mikal. You don't look a day over thirty-eight."

Best friend. I heard him say it. *Best friend . . .*

SHERRY NICOLAS WAS NINETEEN years old when she came into our lives. She had just started at university with nothing in the world but a fake ID, a few changes of clothes, and a really large poster of Marilyn Monroe. And a couple of smaller posters of James Dean, a young Brando, and a framed postcard of Steve McQueen. She grew up in that part of the burbs that used to be the country not too long ago. This was her first time ever away from home. We were her first new friends. It's hard to know how to feel.

WE RETURNED TO RICHARD'S apartment with the new girl in tow and you'd have never known we had left. Skrewdriver blasted on the stereo. The drunks were belligerent. Some people were making out. Some appeared to be fighting. Some appeared to do both. Slamming, pilin'-on, diving from the speakers. This baldie Neanderthal I only ever knew as "Meat Cake" was swinging a girl around by her neck. We'd

seen them do this countless times before. She would scream
and cry but if you tried to put a stop to it she'd kick you in the
nuts. Whatever. Some shirtless maniac tossed Foster's oilcans
to us all immediately upon arrival. Sherry looked wide-eyed
and taken aback by all the goings-on . . . but something told
me she'd seen her share of rip-snortin' hoedowns before. Suzi
jumped on my back and doused me with beer. She squealed
as I spun in circles swinging her around, her boots whacking
some poor sucker in the teeth. Brian and Joe smashed beer
cans against their foreheads and dove into the swirling whirl-
pool of bodies. And so went the remainder of my seventeenth
birthday in much the same fashion. After a while Richard
and Sherry disappeared. Surprise.

Once the last of the folks had either passed out or gone
home Suzi and I retired to our little nest on the screened-in
back porch. For my birthday Richard had given me a futon
mattress from his parents' house. That night I finally brought
Suzi to orgasm for the first time. Or perhaps she just faked it
on account of my birthday. Either way . . .

"I want you to come meet Daddy this weekend," she said
lazily as she drifted off to sleep. "I know you'll really like him.
He's the most coolest-est."

"Okay, if that's what you want."

"I promise the wicked witch won't be there," she said,
yawned, and then fell into instant deep sleep. I pulled the
blanket down a bit from her bare back to inspect the series of
what looked like razor cuts along her shoulder blade. "Cold,"
she whined, and pulled the blanket back up. That's just the
way it was.

I GOT UP FOR a glass of water and some aspirin sometime before daybreak. Walking out into the kitchen I heard
the unmistakable sound of Wagner's *Die Meistersinger von
Nüremberg* spinning on the turntable in Richard's bedroom.

That was no surprise. I was also not taken aback by the sound of Sherry Nicolas gasping, panting, and moaning Richard's name. What instead bashed into me from nowhere was my own reaction to it. I instantly crumpled to my knees and covered my ears as tightly as I could. My stomach twisted into knots and a cold sweat broke out on my brow. *But why?* I'd overheard Richard poke plenty of broads on numerous occasions. At the absolute worst it was only ever vaguely annoying. But listening to this girl cry, "I c-c-can't believe . . . I can't buh-be-believe . . . you're fucking me! Oh god, you're FUCKING me!!!" . . . it carved into to my chest like an ice pick. It ripped me to shreds. It was too real. *Too naked.* Too close. *I can't be here now. I'm not supposed to be here now. I didn't mean to be where I'm not allowed* . . . But why?

Back out on our porch, Suzi whispered to me, "Are they still goin' at it?"

"Yeah," I chuckled, taking my best stab at nonchalance. I must have failed miserably.

"What's wrong, Mikal?"

"Huh? Ain't nothin' wrong, of course. Go back to sleep, Suze."

"Did you have a good birthday?"

"Yeah, I did. Of course I did. Of course."

FOUR

When I awoke the next morning Suzi was gone. Off to school. There wasn't a woman in the house. I came out to the main room to find a bunch of the boys sitting around inspecting handguns. Richard sat frowning at his framed issue of *Völkischer Beobachter* from 1920, which normally hung on the wall in the hallway. The glass was shattered. I gave him a sympathetic look. He shrugged.

"No big deal. The frame itself is fine. Well worth it for the party we had. Get dressed, Mikey. We're going down to the range for practice."

"I don't have a gun," I said.

"For real, Mike?" Joe exclaimed. "And you were living in Niggerville? Goddamn. You must have a death wish, boy."

"We'll get you a piece," Richard said. "Everybody needs a pistol."

"I don't want a gun," I said flatly. "I ain't going."

"Hmm . . . ," Richard grunted, nodding. "Apparently you misheard me. When I said, 'We're going down to the range for practice,' it must have sounded to your ears like, 'If you think it might be a peachy keen afternoon, would you like to maybe join us?' Reasonable enough mistake, but hear me clearly now. WE. ARE. GOING. TO THE RANGE. FOR PRACTICE."

"Hear me clearly," I replied. "I. AIN'T. GOING." And I turned around and went back to the porch.

As I got dressed, I figured that that was the end of my tenure as a ground soldier in the Racial Holy War. Dishonorable discharge.

After a few minutes Richard came out to the porch and sat on a stack of cushions. He didn't appear angry. He just sat and waited for me to explain myself. When I didn't he finally said, "Okay, let's hear it. What's your deal with the guns?"

"They're just not for me. I don't like 'em."

"A gun is just a tool, Mike. Nothing to be afraid of."

"I ain't afraid. I just don't do guns."

"A tool, you hear me? Like a hammer or a drill."

"I don't do hammers or drills neither."

"Dude, I've seen you use chains and blackjacks. I know you carry a switchblade. What's the fucking difference?"

"YOU KNOW GODDAMN WELL WHAT THE GODDAMN DIFFERENCE IS!"

"Mike," Richard said calmly, "tell me what's on your mind."

We sat still in another round of silence. "You know," I finally said, "it's hard to know how to feel when your best friend blows out a man's stomach with a shotgun . . ."

I told him all about my buddy in Louisville. I told him about Blackchurch and the overabundance of firearms. Going to sleep every night to the *rat-tat-tat*. I told him about watching the boy get shot in the temple and the thigh right in front of me. I told him, in no uncertain terms, I don't do guns. He listened attentively, never interrupted or interjected. When I had said my piece, he replied, "Anybody ever pull one on you?"

"Yeah. Some nig put a rod to the back of my head behind Sunny Mart."

"Did he rob you?"

"No, he just said, 'Is you scared?' I said, 'Yep.' He left it there for a couple of minutes, poking into my skull, just to make me sweat. Then he laughed and walked away."

"Huh. Just showing off his big black cock."

"I guess."

"But see, he would have had no power over you if you'd had a big black cock of your own to point back at him."

Touché.

"Rich, I've said what I'm gonna said about this. If you want me to leave I'll leave right now. But I will *never* carry a gun. Even if that means I'll die for being outgunned."

"You're not leaving," he said. "I've heard you out, and I don't agree with your position . . . but I respect it. You can hang out here today. We'll be back around six and we'll all go get some steaks or something." And that was that.

STAYING HOME ALONE ALL morning and afternoon turned out to be a great decision simply for its own sake. It hadn't occurred to me until then, but since joining this crew, virtually all of my waking life had been spent with them. It was an unexpectedly welcome relief to just hang out with myself inside my own head for a couple of hours. I played a bunch of Richard's rare vinyl on the vintage turntable. I ordered a pizza with banana peppers, which I could normally never do since Brian was allergic to them. I played video games. Just because I felt that I probably should, I took a stab at reading *Mein Kampf*, which has got to be the single most skull-meltingly boring book ever written.

I was mightily disappointed when I heard the front door open and somebody inquire, "Anybody home?" It was Sherry Nicolas.

"In here," I said, not taking my eyes off *Sonic the Hedgehog*.

She came in, dropped her book bag in the corner, kicked her shoes off next to it, and peeled off her socks. She sat down next to me Indian-style on the obliterated couch.

"*Sonic?*" she asked.

"The very same. You wanna play?"

"Nah. You here alone?"

"They're shooting."

"Guns?"

"No, they're shoo—yes . . . guns."

"My brothers and my dad all hunt. I don't care for guns myself."

"Just a tool. Like a hammer or a drill. Nothing to be scared of."

"Guess you're right. I was feeling special cuz Richard gave me a key to y'all's pad, but then I found that the front door was unlocked anyway."

"We never lock it. We're actually hoping some jungle bunnies try to come in and take shit. That would be good times. Don't let that stop you from feeling special, though."

"Richard gets a lot of girls, doesn't he?" she asked, jumping straight to it. Knocked me off balance for a moment.

"Not really," I lied. "You see a bunch of other broads with keys milling around in here?" There was a long pause that I tried to not let distract from the game. But it drove me nuts and I finally said, "So, uh, how is it? College, I mean?"

And out it came a-flooding . . .

"Too much. You know what I mean? It's just too damn much. I'm always lost, always late, always short of money. Like college like life, right? Always have the wrong book, always in the wrong room at the wrong time. Back and forth, back and forth, office to office: Bursar, Registration, back to Admissions, Financial Aid. My name magically disappears from class lists. 'It's NICOLAS! N-I-C-oh never mind.' I don't know anybody and nobody wants to know me. Everyone had already been picked for teams and I didn't even know what we were playing."

"I hear ya."

"And when I finally do get to class it's all . . . screeching. Agenda versus agenda. Before I hopped the bus to get here, my brothers joked that I'd need to beware for all the 'commie fag liberals' on campus. Ha ha. But hell, I think I could DEAL with those . . . whatever they are. I can't ever get a word in edgewise, and even if I could I wouldn't have anything to say. 'You there! Helen Keller. What do you think about the plight of blah blah blah and the rising cost of suchnsuch.' Uuuuhhhh . . . And the steamroller just flattens me and rolls on. I don't matter. I'm invisible."

"Yeah?"

"Yeah . . . ," she said, absently fiddling with her ankle bracelet. "Richard sees me, though."

"Hm."

"I like Richard . . . a lot."

"So I heard," I said. I could almost feel her face scorch up bright scarlet. It singed my shoulder.

"Oh my god . . . ," she gasped. "I am so embarrassed now."

"I'm just kiddin' with you," I lied again. "I ain't hear nothing."

"You're lying. I can tell. You're lying to make me feel better. But I know you heard me last night. Ohhhh god." She buried her face in her hands.

"I got up to get a few aspirin at some point and I vaguely heard a bit of rustling around. Y'all coulda been rearranging furniture for all I know."

"Really?" she asked meekly.

"If I'm lyin' I'm dyin'."

"I like your tattoos."

"Do they look familiar?"

"I'mma get a beer, 'kay? You want one?"

"Be careful. There might be broken glass in the hallway."

"I'm in my bare feet a lot. Ah'm jest uh lil ole cuntreh gurl," she said in a horribly affected hick accent. I laughed obligatorily.

When she returned she handed me a beer and said, "I'm hungry. You guys have any eatables? Didn't see anything."

"There's some ground beef in the freezer," I said. "That's about it."

"I'm a vegetarian," she replied. "I can't even be anywhere near beef or I will get horribly sick to my stomach."

"Well, welcome to Shit Creek. I hope you brought your own paddle."

"You got a car?"

"No. You?"

"Nope. God, we're pitiful."

"There's a grocery right out the backyard if you wanna pick up something."

"You reading *Mein Kampf*?"

"Tried to."

"Boring as hell, isn't it?"

"Boy howdy."

"I really like reading about, like, Hollywood Babylon–type stuff. All the dirt and la-di-da about old Hollywood."

"How old?"

"Old old. Like 1950s. And even earlier." She paused contemplatively for a moment, then said, "Richard's kinda got a bit of a 'young Brando' thing about him. Mixed with maybe Douglas Fairbanks." I didn't know who the second guy was. I still don't, actually.

"Not James Dean?" I asked.

"Dean was queer, you know," she said. That hung in the air like a small cloud for a moment as I tried to figure out where it came from. Inexplicably, she followed it with, "Richard gave me a bunch of vinyl records."

"To keep?" I asked, genuinely astonished.

"Uh huh!" she chirped brightly, figuring out from my tone that this was indeed something of note.

"And you're feeling special about the key? Pffffft. What did he give you?"

"The first Bad Brains record," she answered beaming. "It's actually a pre-print I guess. Or some sort of alternate release. The cover's different and it's got different takes of a couple of songs."

"No way! What did he say when he gave it to you?"

"He said, 'Those niggers were pretty good until they went metal.'"

"I think they're pretty fucking awesome regardless—now, then, and forever."

"Me too," she said. "I think you and I have a lot in common. He gave me bit of classic stuff: Minor Threat, the Dead Boys, Sick Of It All. He insisted I take some other stuff like Final Solution—"

"OI!" I shouted.

"All right, they're good I take it. Okay. He gave me a 7-inch of some group called The Hangmen."

"We actually know those guys. If you're going to be around you'll meet them soon enough. Craaaaazy fuckers. I think they're all inbred. I watched their lead singer eat a dead squirrel one time."

"Ewwwwwww!"

"I swear. We was at a rally on this farm way out in Deliverance country. They played. Some other bands played. I guess this squirrel had tried to jump from the garage to the house and bit into a power line. It had been hanging there from its teeth for like two weeks. So Goat Skinner, that's what everybody calls him, pulls it off the line and chomps right into it. He claimed it was cooked."

"Charming."

"That's just the way it is."

"This music," she asked, ". . . this is all racist stuff, right?"

"*Racialist.*"

"Okay. Sorry."

"It's the soundtrack for the revolution."

"The revolution . . . when white people finally take control?"

"Well," I said, annoyed, ". . . that's a pretty . . . simplistic way to put it."

"I just don't do hate all that well," she said.

"You know what? I don't really do hate myself. And Richard

really don't neither. We're kind of different from other racialists in that way. There's a lot of unfocused aggression in the White Power movement. You'll hear a bunch of people shouting RAHOWA, Racial Holy War, and it's a nice little football chant. But I kind of think—I hope—it ain't necessary. It's like when you hear these rich punk rock kids scream about 'anarchy.' What, and give up that BMW Daddy done bought you? Gets frustrating sometimes, but ultimately it's good to have your troops single-minded of purpose without a lotta, you know, complexities in their thinking. And stuff."

"So where are you guys coming from?"

"We're all about going back to a very simple premise that was good in the past and is still good: complete racial segregation. So-called ethnic diversity is a tragically failed experiment, and it's time for it to end. It is human nature to want to be with your own kind. Chicanos want to be with other Chicanos. Japanese want to be with Japanese. Forcing everyone together in a pot and saying, 'Okay! Melt!' has only led to violence, misery, confusion, and racial impurity for everyone involved. Being that the U.S. is a predominantly white country, we think everybody else needs to go home. Or we can split up the country. Don't make me no nevermind."

"Wow. That's intense." She flipped the tab on her can and blew into the opening, trying to get a tone. She continued, "It does make sense, though. I always think it's so sad when I see mulatto kids. Like, where do they belong? What's their identity? How could people not think about that before they have those children?"

I nodded and said, "How that ain't considered child abuse straight off I'll never know. Believe me, I lived the experiment. It's a failure. My parents live in a mostly colored neighborhood. I used to live with them there. Blacks, left entirely on their own, shoot each other up like it's a game. I've watched them do it right in front of me. You add Caucasians to the mix, you add gooks to the mix, and now everybody's gotta 'posse up.' It's madness, and it needs to end."

"Look at me," she said. "Fresh into town, and I sought you guys out right away."

"There you go. Everybody wants to be with their own kind. There was a dude in my old neighborhood who became a Black Nationalist, back-to-Africa type. Senbe Shabazz. He called multiculturalism 'pollutin' and dilutin'.' I tell you, I couldn't stand the son-of-a-whore personally, but I agreed with everything he stood for."

"Except," she said, "that he felt that blacks are superior to everyone else. Right?"

"That's cool. Everyone thinks their group is the best one. Fuck, every tribe of American Indian's name for themselves translates in their tongue as 'The True People.' But," I couldn't help but grin, "WE ain't called the Master Race for no reason." Sherry laughed and nodded. "Speaking of Indians," I continued, "I got nothing but respect for them people. They got it right. They keep to themselves in their own communities and maintain their own culture. There's the 'business model,' as Richard says."

"I tell you what, y'all would hate what I see on campus every day. It's like one big Benetton ad."

"I've seen that shit. Queers, kikes, cripples, rag heads, all hanging around together holding hands pretending to buy the world a Coke. That's why Richard dropped out and why I'm never going."

"I was wondering why you're not in school."

"I was expelled. For trying to teach some shaved apes a lesson in reality. There was a lot of hooting and shit-throwing, I'll tell you that much."

"You've got . . . quite a vocabulary for slurs."

"It's a talent, not a gift."

"Well, I don't know about 'The Revolution,' but . . . I'd like to see a revolution where more than one opinion—read:

liberal secular opinion—is allowed at college. It's out of control. My first day of Women's Studies and there's this wacko-left freak in class . . . a *man* mind you . . . hollering at a bunch of feminists for *not being feminist enough*."

"Ha ha! For all their bullshit about tolerance, they're not even tolerant with each other."

"And there's this black chick everybody's ga-ga over. Oh, she's soooo great. She's just some homegirl with a big mouth, but you'd think she was the fucking Empress of Ethiopia."

"Of course. Gotta reward every little thing they do."

"And just today I had the nerve to mention God in class, and you would have thought I was force-feeding the body of Christ down people's throats."

"You Catholic?"

She paused nervously then said, "You all hate Catholics, don't you."

I laughed.

"We're not The Klan," I said. "I ain't got a problem with Catholics. Pope Pious, one of them, was a big supporter of the Third Reich. At least that's my understanding."

"I didn't know that."

"How could you know? They're not going to teach that in school. That's not politically correct. It might make people ashamed of their religion, or worse yet, might make them stop to think that maybe Hitler wasn't the monster they've been forced to believe he was. Either way it's another symptom of the . . . infantilization of our culture. That's why we have to fight."

"Infantilization?"

"You know what I mean. Babyfication . . . somethin'."

She giggled, "That's so funny, what you do with your voice."

"What? What do you mean?"

"When it's just you talking, it's all '*mumble mumble fuckin' mumble grumble*.' But then when you go on a tear about THE

BIG ISSUES, Professor Mikal steps up to the podium. I just think it's funny. The two yous."

"Hmmm. Yeah . . ."

I had completely lost interest in the adventures of everyone's favorite digital vermin, so I shut the TV off. We sat in silence for a moment. After a bit, Sherry asked, "So . . . if I join you guys, if you'll let me, do I have to wear those big old steel-toed boots like you're wearing?"

I shrugged. "You never know when you gotta kick somebody."

"I just don't like my feet to be imprisoned. A lot of the girls were barefoot last night."

"Psh. Shows their dedication," I said in mock disdain. *Surely she can tell I'm joking with her.* If she could, it didn't show.

"Well," she said warily, "I hope I can stay around. I mean, Richard seemed to, you know . . . enjoy me." My stomach immediately locked up again. "I'm sorry," she continued, blushing afresh, "I don't know what I'm talking about."

JUST THEN THE BOYS came bursting through the door like a herd of wildebeests.

"Hey you," Sherry cooed to Richard, her voice suddenly regressing to a very high, little-girl timbre. "I know you!"

Richard scooped her up off the couch and gobbled on her neck. She squealed and kicked her legs in the air. He deposited her back onto the couch next to me. She kissed his fingers as he slid his hand across her cheek. I could have done without all of that.

"How'd it go?" I asked the assembled mob.

"Killer," said Joe. "We're ready to slaughter people."

"Sweet."

"Yer a fag, Mikey," Geoff announced.

"Really? Is that why I fucked your mother up the ass last night?"

"Yep. Cuz she's a fag hag. Did you draw a hairy chest on her back?"

"I sure did."

"You guys are messed up," said Sherry.

"Duly noted."

"Goddamn," Brian said sniffing. "Were there banana peppers in here? I swear to fucking god just being in this room I'm gonna swell up and die."

"Are you going to explode and splatter all over the place?" Phil asked him. "Cuz if you are, then I gotta leave. These are my good pants."

"If you die can I have your skateboard?" I asked.

"No, cuz you killed me, fucker."

"Why you gotta hold a grudge?"

"Anyway," Richard cut in, "if you niggers are done with Showtime at the Apollo, I'm starving."

"Red meat," Phil said chomping his teeth. "Thick, raw, and menstruating. That's what we need." A chorus of "Hell yes" chimed all around the room.

"What do you say, Sherry?" Richard asked, brushing a few golden strands away from her eyes. "Hungry for anything in particular?"

"Um . . . ," Sherry replied, "red meat sounds great to me."

FIVE

That weekend Suzi and I went to meet her father. Her eyes lit up like Christmas morning when he came strolling in and she kissed him on the cheek with a loud smacker.

We met at a local greasy spoon because Suzi's mother was home sick with the flu and nobody wanted to be there for that. Suzi had been taking care of her mom to the best of her abilities, bringing her soup and orange juice and whatnot. I guess something or other had enraged the lady, though, because Suzi's lip was split and fattened on one side and her chin was bruised. Something about a flying vomit bucket and I really didn't want to hear any more.

"It was an accident," her father said. "Her mother didn't mean to hurt her."

We ran out of conversation pretty quickly. I don't think Old Man was too impressed with me, not that he had much reason to be, and I'd have to say the feeling was mutual.

"Nice haircut, Mick."

"Mike."

"Mike."

Nothing struck me as particularly wrong about him, but he was no cause for celebration as far as I could see. I couldn't help but think, *Why are you letting this happen? Why are you allowing your daughter to be brutalized?*

"You got a job, Mike?"

"Sort of."

"What do you do?"

"Well . . . um . . ."

If you really loved her, you know . . . you wouldn't . . . you wouldn't . . .

AFTER DINNER SUZI AND I said farewell to Father of the Year and went down to Eldon's Tavern to see a local bluegrass singer named Jasper Highway. The rest of our gang was elsewhere that night, and it was good to be alone. El gave us each a soft drink and said, "No back talk, you two. Yer lucky I let yuz in."

"Isn't Daddy every bit as great as I said?" Suzi asked me.

Jasper sang, *"I got a heartache, love, deeper than the sea . . ."*

"Yeah," I said. "Uh huh. Absolutely."

If you really loved her . . .

THAT NIGHT WE TRIED to have sex in the shower, but it was too slippery and awkward and by the time we got to bed Suzi said she felt dizzy and fell right to sleep. I heard Richard and Sherry stumble in through the front door and head straight into his bedroom. Suzi rolled over and wrapped her arms around me from behind. I held her hands to my chest and kissed her fingers.

"Mikal . . ." she whispered, half-asleep.

"Yeah?"

"Could you get me a glass of water?"

Goddamn it . . . The last place in the world I wanted to be right then was out in that kitchen . . . except for possibly the room adjoining.

"Awww . . . ," I grumbled. "I'm comfortable. Go back to sleep."

"I'm thirsty!"

I mumbled something incoherent in reply and she rolled back over.

"Jeez. What a gentleman YOU are. I'll just go get it myself." And she stomped out into the kitchen. Half a minute later she came back out to the porch and said, "Holy Christ, you should hear—"

"I don't want to hear about it."

RICHARD HAD PICKED UP a temp job working on an assembly line and I was looking for something myself so I could start pulling my own weight around the house rentwise. It was a Monday afternoon and I was sitting in the living room poring over the Employment page when Sherry came in dragging an old ghost behind her.

"Mikal, I met THE scariest dude ever today. Well, I can't really say I met him cuz I already had seen him cuz he's in my Women's Studies class, right? I told you about that. But anyway, there's this girl in that class named Paige. She's hardly ever there. But when she is there all she does is cause fights. Everybody calls her the Raging Bull-dyke, which is fairly right-on except I think she's actually probably kind of pretty in her own way. Like, imagine young Elvis if he was a woman and had pine-green hair."

"Uh . . . Okay . . ."

"Anyway, she's really laying into the rest of the women and I'm staying out of it, of course. She's saying shit like, 'You can't go slurping the enemy's goop and then whine when he doesn't call you the next day,' and all sorts of crap about men that I didn't really understand. And Creepy Guy, he's her friend, he's just sitting there loving it, soaking it all in. But when people start to fight back against Paige he chimes in with all this stuff about 'Sojourner Truth,' and 'Susan B. Whatsherface,' and this other chick goes, 'What right do you have to criticize? Are you a woman? Do you have a vagina?' And he snarls at her, 'You mean besides the one I keep in the mason jar?'"

With that, got to admit, I snorted beer out of my nose.

"Everyone freaks out, right? Bull-dyke Paige is cracking up laughing, and the prof tells the freak to get out. It was CRAZY."

"Fuckin' hell."

"Dude and Paige, they've got this whole circle of friends that are just like that . . . you remember the Benetton ad? 'Kikes and queers and rag heads' and all. Well, later I run into the guy in the elevator. He held the door for me, which was actually really kinda nice of him because I was running late and I had papers spilling out of my arms.

"'So hey,' I said, trying to be friendly, 'you're in my Women's Studies class, right? Seems like a pretty interesting one, yeah?' And he just starts growling, 'Bunch of fucking June Cleavers in that class. Get thin, get sexy, get a rich man. That's what passes for liberation at the end of the millennium.' Or words to that effect. And I'm just a stuttering idiot, talking about, 'Oh . . . well . . . umm . . .'

"'Goddamn *Cosmo* cunts,' he says. 'It's programming, you see what I'm saying? *YM* to *Jane* to *Cosmo* to *Good Housekeeping.* Everybody laps it up. They want the program.' And I'm just staring at my feet, wishing the stupid elevator would hurry the hell up so I could get off. He keeps going, 'Cuz, you see, true freedom's just too hard. All the Bettys have now decided that cleaning house, watching Home Shopping, and fucking the mailman ain't such a tough gig. You rushing?' He points at the sorority postings I had crumpled in my hand. I had no intention of rushing, I just picked them up for the heck of it.

"But he says, 'Yeah, I used to think all those people needed to be lined up and executed, but hey, if date rape and paid-for friendship is your bag, who am I to complain?' The doors FINALLY open and he steps out. Doesn't even turn around, but says, 'Keep your head up. It's sink or swim. Welcome to university life.' Then he disappeared down the hall. I'm all, 'Nice talking to you.' To nobody. Christ."

"What's the guy look like?" I asked her. Even though I already knew.

"Like the devil. Absolutely COVERED in these viney, like, abstract tattoos. Not cool, spare ones that actually mean something, like yours. 'Tribal' I guess you'd call them. And even though it is hotter than the Congo out there today he's layered in clothes like it's Minnesota in January. Leather and flannel. Yeesh. And his hair . . . is down to his ass, twisted and knotted into the most gnarliest dreadlocks I've ever seen on a white boy or anybody. Like they were dyed with animal blood or something."

"That's what I thought," I said. "He doesn't just look like the devil. He *is* the devil."

"You know him?"

"I've guessed his name." *Jack Curry* . . .

I didn't say anything more. *I hate the guy. Hate him.* It was that visceral, caveman hate. That hate that sits on you because it can never land on its intended target. Like being in the ocean with a nosebleed and hating sharks. Like hating cancer.

"Well . . . anyway," Sherry said to fill the empty space, "I'm excited. It's my first farm rally tonight!"

Her excitement was justified. There was a tangible electricity on the farm that night. Sherry was disappointed at first that The Hangmen weren't playing, as they'd been hyped up so much leading up to the day. Alas, their drummer had been jailed for burning down a black Baptist church. In their place was some grunt-core band called Confront whom everybody else seemed to like, but I thought were boring. As far as I could tell, all their songs were called either "Run Nigger Run" or "Die Nigger Die." In fact I think they played "Die Nigger Die" three times in a row, but I'm not sure how one could tell.

THANKFULLY RICHARD WAS THERE to bring it all home.

HE TOOK TO THE stage *after* the band for a change, the headliner you could say, and I could tell that he had a new spark about him that night. Something had stoked the fire. It wasn't anything glaring or excessive. Just a spark. I could sense that it wasn't going to be the usual "Destroy," "Maim," "Kill them all" skinhead bullshit that night. That night he had a brighter burn.

He began, "A famous colored man once said, 'Move over, or we will move over you.'" Guffaws from the crowd. "Sorry, Stokely." Laughter and jeers . . . though a number of folks had to explain it to their friends. "Although I appreciate the gumption and gusto, he didn't have the power." Pause. Then, "WE . . . have the power." Cheers and shouts of "White Power!" rose as if on cue. "We are the power. I think it goes without saying, but in order to be a true revolutionary, you must fight for what you love and love what you're fighting for. I know I do. I love my race, and even more so, I love my country." There was a smattering of claps. "And that's why I fight for them." Clapping and cheering. *Where's he going?* I wondered. I knew that he knew, but would the crowd follow? "I know a lot of Skins are down on America these days. They resent the welfare system. They get all pissy about the lip service paid to 'equality,' 'inclusiveness,' the whole 'open society' catastrophe and all that." Groans and hisses. I chuckled to myself. "Hell, some of us are still sour because America took Hitler out." Laughter and whistling. Richard played with the tension and uncertainty of his audience. Teasing and coaxing when needed, grabbing and throttling when it's not expected. "But I'm here to say that I love America. I'm proud that the U.S. took down Hitler's regime. Don't get me wrong, I have great admiration for Hitler. He's a hero of mine; you know that." Applause. "He did what was right for his people in his time. You must admire that. But he made a lot of mistakes . . . and he fell short of the glory." Silence. Only the crickets had a retort, and it went unnoticed. "America can learn from the mistakes of the Third Reich. And we will. And we are. I love America." Cheers. "I'm proud to be American. I'm proud to be a part of America's new golden age, which is just around the corner, people. Just around the corner. The pieces are in place. The gears are already working. The war is already on." Shouts of RAHOWA! began to burst out from pockets of the crowd. Richard dropped the microphone to his side for a moment, grinning and nodding as more and more people hollered RAHOWA! RAHOWA! RAHOWA!!! "We have friends in important places," he continued. "Know that. As we speak, our friends are chiseling away at the communist 'New Deal' leftovers. They're dismantling that toxic doctrine 'multiculturalism' that pollutes our society with a cloud of fake togetherness that is neither necessary nor desired." Cheers and applause. "They are yanking away the free lunches from the lazy and the weak. America will move again. WE are going to get America moving again. I'm proud to be a part of it. I LOVE America." Hearty cheering and shouting. "Old Glory is the new swastika and I am proud to salute her!" An explosion of cheers and applause broke out. "Mark my words, in the next ten years America will succeed where Hitler failed. Fat Willie and his hog dyke wife are a dead breed and we will dump them on the curb with the rest of the waste and America will at last take its rightful place in this world. The Third Reich has passed. The Fourth Reich is in America right now ready

to pull out the aces. The Fifth Reich . . . is *us*." A deafening
roar rose up from the crowd. The stars and the moon above
were outshone by the light of Richard's eyes. "We are the
power." A deep guttural chant of WHITE POWER filled the
air. It rumbled in the ground and shook the trees. I squeezed
Suzi's hand. She wrapped her arms tight around my bicep
and lay her head on my shoulder. Sherry watched Richard
onstage. Enraptured. WHITE POWER. WHITE POWER.
Richard saluted "sieg heil" with his hand and mouthed "God
Bless America." *WHITE POWER. Sieg heil. God Bless America. WHITE POWER. Sieg heil. God Bless America* . . .

FROM THE MOMENT RICHARD stepped off the stage
Sherry was attached to his arm like a barnacle on a ship's
hull. As many of the folks began to trickle away, a number of
us relocated inside the farmhouse, keeping the fire alive. It
was very late, and most of us were drunker than we had really
intended to get. Suzi sat on my lap whispering all the things
she planned to do to me once we got home, none of which
we ever got around to.

At some point Brian walked in the door dragging this
grungy dirthead with a black toolbox by his neck. *Hell yes* . . .
Screwtape, everybody's favorite tat man.

"Hey!" Brian shouted. "Lookit what I almost stepped in!"
Everyone hollered approval.

"I'll be in the kitchen," Screw announced, "if anybody
needs a touch-up."

A few of us muscled our way in quickly. Guys proceeded
to pull off their shirts, girls peeled off fishnets, sleeves rolled.
The room was an ocean of ink-stained flesh. Sherry stumbled
drunkenly into the kitchen.

"I want one! I want one!" she slurred.

Screw sneered at her, "Better clear it with your daddy first,
little girl."

A few people chuckled.

"Eat me, you faggot!" Sherry snapped at him. Screw jumped back, startled. Those of us who sort of knew her were taken aback as well. It was certainly a side we hadn't seen as yet. We all howled with laughter, and called Screw out as a pussy for his concern. Sherry yanked her shirt up, exposing her breasts to all in attendance and pointed to the swastika on Richard's shoulder. "I want this, right here over my fucking left tit, see!"

Screwtape grimaced and looked at Richard, unsure of what to do.

"Better do what you're told, Screw." Richard chuckled.

"Rich," he pleaded. "Come on. She's drunk as hell. She's gonna bleed like a cherry on prom night."

Richard shrugged and guzzled the remainder of his beer.

"Come on, Tape," I said. "Your reputation's on the line."

"Take a message," he said with a shrug of resignation.

Screw pulled out his needle gun, cranked up the buzz. I stood right behind Sherry, and I heard him whisper in her ear . . .

"Listen to me carefully, okay? If anyone asks you what this is, tell 'em it's a sun wheel, you hear me? A sun wheel. That's all. Or . . . tell 'em you're Hindu."

I barely stifled a laugh, but Sherry just nodded, hardly able to keep her balance. As Screwtape pressed the buzzing needle against her skin she gave out a little whimper of pain, but held strong, determined to see it through. See it she did not, however, for as soon as the first trickle of blood dripped from her bare nipple, she blacked out and collapsed backward into my arms. I held her up as vertical as I could while Screw finished the piece. Once it was completed, Richard relieved me of her. He scooped her up to carry her out to the car. Laughing, he rolled his eyes, and kissed the top of my bristly head in gratitude. *All in a day's work.*

Once we got home we all crashed hard. Reeba and Phil

had pretty well commandeered the abandoned apartment next door and a number of people fell out over there.

As I lay down to go to sleep, Suzi said, "Mikal, let's pretend like we're gonna get married someday, okay?"

"Why pretend?"

"I'd like to meet your folks sometime."

"No you wouldn't. Trust me."

"I bet you're coloring them unfairly. Why do you think they love your brother more than you?"

"Because I lived."

SIX

The next morning I was awakened by clumsy rustling out in the living room. I walked in to see Sherry frantically stuffing papers and books into her school bag. She was decked out: tight Final Solution T-shirt, black boots with "RAHOWA," "white power," and all the necessaries painted on, jeans she must have been stitched into, and a leather tie-off wrapped around her wrist (which I found out later was some bit of a "game" between herself and Richard). I had never really noticed her figure before then. It was indeed worth noticing. She grabbed Richard's jacket, which was too big for her, zipped it up, and rolled down the cuffs of her jeans to cover anything potentially offensive or controversial. She smiled thinly to me. I could tell she was hungover and hating the morning sun like all hell. I was pretty well there myself, but at least I didn't have Beginning Calculus at 9:00 AM.

"Thanks for saving me last night," she said. "I guess I woulda gone splat on the tiles if you hadn't been there to catch me."

"What are friends for," I said. She nodded.

"Reeba's gonna do my hair tonight. I'm thinking maybe a Siouxsie Sioux–meets–Annie Lennox sort of look. What do you think? Pretty rad, huh?"

"I don't know who that is," I said. I still don't. Never did keep up with old Hollywood.

"Reeba says she's gonna make me look super hot. I've never looked super hot before."

"Good luck with that."

"Quite a commitment on my part I guess," she said, indicating her new look.

I laughed. "The real commitment is, as we speak, scabbing up on your left boob."

"God, it itches so badly," she whined.

"Don't scratch it, you'll fuck it up. When you get home from school put some lotion on it. You'll be all right."

"We'll see," she said, and headed out on her way. "Hey Mikal," she said, turning back again. "Did you know that Hitler was a vegetarian?"

"I did indeed, yes. Raised Catholic too."

She smiled and walked out. *Whatever it takes.*

RICHARD STAYED IN HIS bedroom the rest of the morning. He must have had a headache rumbling straight from the bowels of the earth, for he did not turn his music on once. I lay on the couch reading most of the day. Considered continuing my search for a job, *but to hell with it.*

AROUND NOON I HEARD the phone ring in Richard's room. He walked it out to the living room where I was, hit the Talk button, and chucked it at me. Amazingly enough, I caught it. He lumbered on back to his room without a word spoken.

"Hello?"

"Is this Mikal?" The woman's voice on the other end was hoarse and desperate. She took a deep drag from her cigarette like it was the last she would ever smoke.

"Yeah."

"This is Suzi's mother."

Well well well.

"How ya doing, Ma? Good to finally hear from ya."

"Listen, I ain't gonna bullshit around here. You takin' Suzi away?"

"Sorry?"

"Are you gonna take her away?!"

So much for getting-to-know-you. I let the moment hang. Figured a little sweating it out is good for the soul. She took another suicide drag from her smoke.

"Well," I answered eventually, "I'd like to, yeah."

"GOOD! You gotta do that. Get her far from here. There ain't nothing for her here."

"So I've noticed. Nothing but a lifetime of ass beatings is how it looks from my angle."

"Look," she said, her voice cracking, "I do what I gotta do. I'm just trying to do what's right. I ain't perfect."

"Uh huh, that's one way of putting it."

"Don't you judge me, you little punk!"

"Listen up, you rancid twat, anything I do, any decision I make, is gonna be because I thought it was the thing to do. Not cuz the likes of you—"

"Goddamn it! Listen to me!"

"D'you hit her in the face with a bucket of—"

"THAT WAS A ACCIDENT!" She started to cry, which just made me angrier.

"You nasty fucking—"

"I heard that you was a smart boy. You don't sound so smart to me."

"Oh, I think I'm smart enough to know what the score is, mother-dear. Let me guess: Your husband don't pay you no mind these days. Marriage ain't been worth a shit for . . . oh, what is it, 'bout sixteen years?"

"You don't get it . . . ," she sobbed.

"Sure, used to be all rose petals and soft music and holding hands in the moonlight, but since you went and squeezed out a baby it just ain't Paris no more. Am I getting warm here?"

"Oh sweet Jesus . . . *sob* . . . you just don't uh-unnerstan' . . ."

"And I guess you're not only resentful, but downright jealous cuz your daughter and your husband have a close bond and ain't nobody got time for poor little you, am I off base? I'm not, am I?"

She just sobbed and muttered, "Just take her away . . . Just take her away . . . Please . . ."

"Okay, Ma, great talking to you. I guess we'll be seeing ya 'round Christmas time."

And I hung up. Richard stuck his head out of his room.

"Who was that?" he asked.

"Mother-in-law."

He nodded and went back in again.

THE BOYS STARTED TO arrive about 2:30 PM and they made so much racket that Richard was finally forced out of bed. He cooked us all up a fat vat of scrambled eggs and sausage. Joe had bought a case of Colt 45, which earned him the name "Jamal" for the remainder of the day. We whiled away our youth playing video games and drinking cheap beer.

Around four Sherry called Richard from school. This is what I heard:

"Uh huh. Uh huh. Holy shit! Goddamn. No way! HA HA! That's wild! Nope. Sure wasn't. I have no idea. Uh uh. If somebody from our chapter or any nearby did it, I'd have known. Whoever it was, I'd like to shake his hand. Naw. I'd shake their hands too. I'd show 'em some luuuv. HA HA! Okay. Okay. You coming over? Okay, see you then. You're gonna what? Wow, that sounds like fun. Is that legal in this state? 'Kay, see you then. Bye."

"What the hell was all that?" I asked after he hung up.

"Somebody apparently trashed the Black Student Union on campus. Somebody spray-painted 'white power' and 'tar babies' all over the place. There was almost a riot, the cops came and everything."

"Was anybody arrested for it?"

"Yeah," Richard said, failing to contain himself. "Two niggers."

I don't remember laughing that long and that hard at any one thing before or since. "Them people just can't catch a break, can they!"

BUT THIS IS WHAT Sherry never told Richard about that day:

SHERRY FOLLOWED JACK CURRY out of class like she did most days, staying far behind. *I couldn't help it, he was like a human car crash. It was impossible to not watch.* Usually he'd be in the midst of some ideological death match with someone or other, but this particular day was pretty quiet. At first.

She took her spot on a bench to eat lunch by herself, watching Curry meet up with his friends under a tree off the main lawn. She didn't know them then, but they were Sarabjit Singh, some girl from the Rape Crisis Center named Marissa, and Lin Cho—who was very pregnant at the time—and her fiancé, Dave Yoshimoto. (You may know of Dave Yoshimoto's sister Katsumi who used to sing for the Baton Rouge sludge metal band Stigmata Dog. She called herself "Pearl Harbor." Perhaps she still does. They were in a horrible accident on Interstate 71 a couple of years ago and most of the band was killed.)

It was a beautiful September day. People were studying, hanging out, grubbing on caf' slop. Jocks tossed the old pigskin around. Hippies Hacky-Sacked. All the little stereotypes frolicked in the sun to and fro; it was an idyllic college scene.

That was the first day that Sherry really noticed Niani Shange. She'd seen her around, as it was hard to see Jack Curry and not see her. They were practically joined at the soul. They lived off campus together in a house nestled back from the road. Niani was something of a star around campus, a champion for all sorts of left-leaning issues. Certainly nothing Sherry wanted anything to do with.

It wasn't difficult to see why people were drawn to her, though: a born performer if ever one lived. She had perfected the art of manipulating her voice for any sized crowd. And I don't care who you are or think you are, there was no denying that she was a stunning sight: incredibly dark, her eyes practically glowed against the deep black of her face. *If a barefoot girl in ripped jeans and a T-shirt could look regal,* Sherry said, *Niani Shange did.* Like a true African queen. She was radiant, and otherworldly gorgeous, and Sherry hated her fucking guts. She hated the respect Niani commanded. She hated the attention Niani received. And for good measure she hated her because Richard would hate her. She and her friends were the perfect poster children for the multicultural agenda. *I'm onto your game, girlie-girl. I'm onto you.* Or so Sherry thought. Sherry had no idea at the time of the devastation Niani would bring. *You could say that I underestimated her. And . . . I suppose, you could blame me for everything that happened.*

Watching Jack and Niani together Sherry was struck by how little they actually talked to one another. Their relationship seemed almost telepathic. Or even *mutually parasitic.*

The afternoon's serenity was broken when a young black man came running across the main lawn, screaming, "Niani! Jack! Awwww hell! This is NOT good!"

THE BLACK STUDENT UNION was in shambles. "Run Nigger Run!" was painted on the walls, along with a few song lyrics with which we had recently become familiar. *Of course*, Sherry said, *my first thought was* Richard. *Richard was my first thought often in those days, but that was the first time that it wasn't accompanied by unmentionable naughtiness.*

Although no one seems sure of the timeline now, it seemed like mere minutes before police were on the scene. Two black men were led away in handcuffs, screaming about injustice, and Jack Curry narrowly avoided getting arrested (or clubbed) himself before Niani grabbed him and pulled him back from the advancing officers. It did seem a tiny bit odd that no one opened, or even *noticed*, the Black Student Union office until one thirty in the afternoon. But Sherry could not give it much thought before she was distracted by the two angry mobs—one white and one black—that had squared off on the center green. No violence—yet. Just a lot of vicious words, and tension so thick it was hard to breathe. The crowd outside of the two mobs watched in anticipation. Sherry stood in that crowd. Along the sides of the buildings, anyone who was neither white nor black kept a smart and safe distance.

Jack Curry and Niani ran through the spectators, splitting a path to the center of it all. Someone pushed Niani and she fell to the ground. A black guy and a white guy instantly started throwing punches at one another and it looked as though a full-scale riot was inevitable. Within seconds Curry smashed both guys in the face and they crumpled to the ground, bloody and unconscious. Everyone gasped and stepped away from Jack Curry as if he were a rabid pit bull. Once again, for a mob, wise thinking.

"Jack! Stop!" Niani screamed, struggling to stand. Sarabjit, Marissa, Dave, and Lin ran to Niani's aid and helped her up. She threw herself immediately into the middle of the closing divide between the black and white crowds.

"Stop!" she yelled at everyone. "You've all got to stop this now!" She continued, ignoring whatever rebuke was coming her way. "I don't know who did that in the center today! And you know what?" Loud grumbling from the mass of people. "I don't care! I don't give a FUCK. It doesn't matter who it was. Whoever they are, y'all sure are making 'em happy! This is exactly what THEY want you to do." A few people shouted, but others quickly shouted them down. She went on, "They played a wack-ass cut, and y'all are dancing to it."

Corny, Sherry thought. But the handful of scattered laughs was enough to shave off a bit of tension. *She knows what she's doing, I guess.*

Niani pointed at a group of Asians all huddled together. "Shit," she said. "If I had known this is what it took to get the Japanese and the Cambodians cuddling, I'd have painted 'white power' up in this bitch my freshman year." Lots of people laughed at that and Sherry instantly thought about what was written on her boots, for once grateful for her inherent invisibility. "Please," Niani said. "We gotta be better than this. Please."

In what has to be a gold-star moment in the history of bad timing, just as things were actually starting to calm, city and county police officers came stomping up the hill in full armor toward the grassy field. Niani screamed, "Everybody please! Run! Hurry! Get back to your classes! Get back to your dorms!" Upon seeing the police, people scattered every which way, knocking each other down in the process. Absolute chaos. Niani stepped toward the encroaching policemen, her palms stretched out toward them.

"No need. No need for that. Everything's peaceful here."

And they . . . retreated. They listened to her.

There were no beatings, no more arrests.

Hmm. Well, Sherry thought, *no denyin' it. That's impressive.*

But any respect that I may have had for that girl just then vanished the moment I saw her later on behind the Fine Arts building . . . sucking face with some alterna-slut.

"You wanna go somewhere?" Niani cooed at the girl, who

nodded like a simp, and they wandered off together hand in hand.

Freaks, Sherry thought. *Fucking gross.* She was sickened. And confused, for she had assumed that Niani Shange and Jack Curry were *together* together. *And if they're not . . . then what was the deal?* It was none of her business.

But she had to find out.

SEVEN

"**M**ikal, change the fuckin' channel, will ya?"

Like a little kid who can't stop picking at a scabbed-up knee, Richard was compelled beyond his will to watch any television program about the "rising scourge of hate crimes in America." He would curse and yell at the TV, holler on and on about the "liberal media" and how "we're being misrepresented."

But the thing is . . . we really weren't. I'll be the first to bitch about the mainstream American media, how they're all bought and paid for, and how they only represent one sanitized point of view. And sure, when they're dealing with the issue of racial "extremism" in America, they can't resist trotting out some toothless flapjack named Buford in a white dress and pointy hat who manages to pull his dick out of his retarded twelve-year-old sister long enough to explain how slavery is justified by the Bible and how whites are the only true humans because we're the only race who can blush. But on the occasion that they deal with Skins, they pretty much nail it. Perhaps they focus too much on the violence and destruction and don't dedicate adequate time to the endless hours spent watching cartoons and pro wrestling, but all in all it's pretty close.

On this particular night, this particular pixelated Buford was in rare form, and Richard expressed God's gift to the white man full tilt by having a whole mess of boiling blood in his face.

"The white race has proved us selves unstoppable!" Buford exclaimed.

"Goddamn . . . the fucking Klan," Richard hissed. "Somebody get me an M16 and I will exterminate them all like the vermin that they are."

Meanwhile, the ladies pretty much ignored the whole affair, as they were busy at work on Sherry's makeover. Reeba and Jennie had cut Sherry's hair very short with chin-length bangs. It was dyed a pronounced maroon with streaks of her natural blond showing through. She did look very hot and I could tell that she wanted Richard to say so. But apart from a smile and a thumbs-ups he never weighed in on the matter. I considered saying something myself, but thought better of it.

After a commercial break a counterpoint was provided by a very severe Panther wannabe in a black beret, who had apparently not gotten the memo that it was no longer 1974.

"No, we do not encourage violence," said Soul Brotha Number One. "No, we do not preach hate. We simply believe that the easiest, quickest, and most logical path towards peace is segregation. We hope to retain the purity of our race, and I would assume whites would like the same for theirs."

"Finally," Richard said. "A man with some basic common sense."

"Tap-dancing porch monkey," Phil sneered. "Go back to Africa, spear chucker!"

Richard chuckled and shook his head. "Settle down, Phil."

"O-bee k-bee, Rich-berd," Phil replied à la Mushmouth. Chuckles all around.

"Just out of curiosity," Richard asked, "any of you guys know what became of the Brown Shirts after WWII?" I was about to answer when Richard held up his finger. He looked around at the rest of them. They weren't even paying attention. "Good. That's what I thought." We looked at each other and grinned. I looked over and saw Sherry watching us intently, as if she wanted in on the joke. *Don't you worry your pretty little head, doll face.*

The phone rang. Joe answered it with a "What," because he's pure class, you see.

"Uh huh," he continued, "Yeah. Hold on. Rich it's uh . . . the, uh . . . Special Olympics." We all snickered like morons. "Um . . . they want to know if you'd consider giving them another . . . er . . . donation."

"Tell them thank you, but I gave all I could last time."

"Awww . . . that's sweet," Sherry said, totally oblivious. Anne began to chime in and Richard made a cut motion across his neck.

"Rich," Joe said. "They're . . . uh . . . crying."

"Hang up, Joey." He did. "Okay," Richard continued, "let's get out of here." That was the last of that.

BARRELING DOWN THE HIGHWAY in Phil's behemoth station wagon, we could not have been any more conspicuous had we been shooting a bazooka out the back window. Swerving all over the road, taunting other drivers, openly drinking beer. An older Chinese couple in a Dodge Colt that should have been dragged out back and shot drove steady and cautious as we cut in front of them. We laughed as the old woman pulled out a rosary and began nodding and chanting. Screeching over to the next lane, we jumped behind them, then sped up and hopped in front of them again. Jennie showed them her tits. The old man gave us the finger. Phil pulled back over side by side with them, and Geoff leaned out the window and spat beer at them screaming, "Bonsai!" (which, admittedly, makes no goddamn sense). The beer

Geoff spat instantly turned to mist about the highway, but I suppose it was the thought that counted. The couple wisely took the next exit and we headed on downtown.

HITTING ALL OF OUR familiar haunts, we tried out a few new joints as well, with varying degrees of success. We ran into trouble for underagedness in a few spots, and I thought Richard was going to destroy this one bartender for grabbing me by my collar and tossing me out the door. (Lucky for that guy he grabbed me and not Sherry.) Everywhere we went someone in our crew would make a comment about who they thought we should stomp, but except for a few dirty looks from a couple of SHARPs, it was pretty mellow most of the night. Had we been serious about looking for ruckus there were several black and Chicano clubs within walking distance whose patrons I'm sure would've been down for a head rumble, but we just never seemed to make it down that way.

"PSSST. MIKAL," SHERRY WHISPERED in my ear as we entered this dingy Industrial club called Lucretia's. "If y'all are serious about wanting to lay somebody out, I'd like to nominate that guy." She indicated a young black fellow at the bar surrounded by white people. We watched homeboy and his Caucasian compatriots do a round of shots, and after he had downed his, he licked a line of salt off the hand of some brunette in a white tank top. "That's Trey McKinley. He's in my Economics class and he is a world-class prick. That girl's name is Melanie, and she's always hanging on him like he's Emperor Jones. It's fucking sickening."

"Yep, that's what we call a 'number one.' I wonder if the rest of the boys have seen him yet."

To this day I'm not sure who it was who started the

number system, but within our crew we always ranked the various stompable offenses one through ten. Number ten escapes me today, but number one was "black man / white woman." I do remember number seven was "Phish fan."

"Jesus, I don't know if I feel like staying at this joint," Sherry said. "It's packed with fuckers from school."

I was just about to ask, *What did you expect?* when I saw a figure exiting the dance floor, slinking toward the bar. Her deep black skin glistened with perspiration that caught the dim lights of the bar just enough to make her shimmer and sparkle. I recognized her . . . but felt I had never seen her before. Ezekial Johnson's little sister. *Niani Shange.* I was so taken with the sight of her for a moment that I hadn't realized that Sherry had completely vanished from the scene. I wasn't one to consider rounded African features or pitch-dark ebony skin in any way attractive. Never. Just not my thing. I choked for a moment when Niani yelled, "Come out and dance with me!" but I quickly realized that she was looking right through me. I didn't exist. And by the time I realized who actually was the intended invitee, I had nowhere to go. *Oh fuck.* Out of the corner of my right eye I saw his multicolored arm slide across the bar to grab a drink, not a millimeter of white skin to be seen amid the tribal twists and smears. A bicycle chain was wrapped around his wrist and held in place by a small padlock. I felt his knotted, natty ropes brush against my jacket. Tied into his hair were what sounded like ball bearings, and they clicked against the bar with a *crrritt, crrritt, crrritt.* I froze up, silently cursing my shaved head. Cursing my red braces. Regretting just for the moment all the conspicuous advertising of my politics and my gang, for these were images I knew he'd recognize, and it wasn't beyond or beneath this psychopath to carve that "white power" right off my neck with a broken bottle.

"Come on, Jack," Niani persisted. "You never dance with me. Just this once."

I'm invisible, I thought. *They don't see me. I'm a phantom. I am bar mist.*

"Be there in a second, Lees," he sighed. "Scout's honor."

She disappeared into a crowd of friends and he, after chugging his drink, followed behind shortly thereafter. Walking past he jabbed me with his elbow, which I immediately thought was a message, but he grunted, "Sorry," and went about his way. *I am invisible.*

Lees? Lisa. That's right . . . her name used to be Lisa. I thought it odd for a moment that he called her by her old Blackchurch name. Odd, because who else in that bar even knew her given name except the two of them and me? *And I don't exist.*

I vaguely heard Joe say, "Can you believe that baboon cunt actually thinks people are looking at her?"

"Yeah," I chuckled. "Gruesome."

AT NO POINT HAD it been discussed, but we all knew where we'd be heading after Lucrecia's. We all simply knew that we would be visiting that section of town most folks called Candyland. Crawling with "number threes."

IT WAS COMING UP on 2:30 AM and most clubs were closing down. We rolled into Candyland just in time to watch the flood of queers spill out into the streets, whooping and singing and prancing about. We pulled into a side alley, shut off the engine, and waited. Some play had just closed at the big theater downtown and many of these people were clearly from that production. Often these folks walked the streets in sizable groups and relocated to after-hours parties at apartment complexes just outside the center of town where parking was relatively safe. *Smart.* But there were always a few stragglers. First dates and out-of-towners and one-night stands eager to get to dessert. That's whom we hunted. That's just the way it was.

Sure enough, separating from the mob were two young dandies holding hands and heading right our way. The one was dressed fairly conservative and, after we exited the wagon and trailed them for a couple of blocks, appeared to me to be a foreigner. English wasn't too strong. Some sort of Eastern European, but I don't know what exactly. The other was American all the way, loud and lit up like Mardi Gras. He wore a huge green feather boa and you could hear his stiletto high heels *click click click*ing down the asphalt from two blocks back. He minced and carried on in this excruciatingly affected high-pitched squeal, periodically calling out to friends across the street as they walked by. Like he was advertising his evening score. Showing off the prize he had won. He cuddled against his new friend and kissed him loudly, calling him either "Jezebel" or "Jessie Bear," I couldn't tell which. All the while we stalked silently behind.

AFTER SOME TIME IT was only them and us, the clamor of downtown somewhere in the distance. Watching the two of them flaunt and advertise I couldn't help but think about where they might be heading and what they would do once they got there. Would they shower together . . . work themselves into a lather, as the saying goes. *Play stupid little faggot games.* The thought of it nauseated me, but I had to dwell on it to get my blood to the right temperature. I had to boil. The more I imagined their costumes and sick little role-playing charades the more I wanted rip their throats out all on my own. Psyching myself up for the justice I was prepared to administer. *Will you put his nuts in your mouth, Queen Bee? What about you, Jezebear, do you welcome that cock into your ass?* I felt the vomit rising in my throat as my fists clenched and my pace quickened. Perhaps had these two gents not been so drunk or so smitten they would have felt the weight of doom pressing harder and harder at their backs as we marched ever closer. Perhaps they would have run or called a friend or the police. But they didn't. And by the time they stopped to make out under a streetlamp, it was simply too late.

"Evening, ladies," Richard said casually. The two of them stared at us for just a moment, mouths agape. Terrified, they huddled together, eyes darting every which way for a possible escape. Queenie squeaked out a pitiful "No" just before we rained down Hell and God's wrath upon them.

The girls had a ritual of their own whenever a stomp was underway. Half of them would laugh and the other half would pretend concern, giving us a finger wag and some vague "now now, that's not very nice" attitude. Who played what role was fluid and ever-changing. That night it was Suzi's turn for the latter. Sherry didn't cop to either, however. She was as blank and uninvolved as if she were standing on the curb waiting for the Metro. Like nothing much was going on at all.

Somehow or another the shrieker became mine and mine alone, the rest of the boys working over the bland foreigner who had rolled himself into a ball begging, "Please . . . to be leaving us . . . now alone, please." Something about the loud one brought out my rage, and the more he pleaded for mercy, the more he sobbed and howled, the greater my contempt grew. *Slam. Smash.* No matter how hard I beat him, though, he wouldn't surrender the act. *Crunch.* He would not lower his register. *Freak! Fucking freak!* He wouldn't drop the pose. *Sick!* He screamed like a woman, cried like a little girl, and all the thrashing in the world would not turn him back into a man.

"Faggot," I muttered as my boot slammed over and over into his abdomen. "Fuck, FUCK him, faggot."

"Please," he whimpered, his lipstick-smeared face awash with blood. "Please . . . don't . . . hurt . . . my baby."

"FUCK HIM!" I yelled, and buried the steel tip of my left boot deep into his rib cage. His forehead smacked the sidewalk and he fell unconscious, still quietly murmuring incoherent pleading, still in a high girl-squeak. A crowd of people several blocks north began charging down toward us, and we darted off, back to the wagon.

It was an unusually somber ride home. I don't know for sure what accounted for the spontaneous contemplative mood. Perhaps Anne summed it up when the silence became more than she could bear and she blurted out, "Fag bashing is God's work. It's holy duty. Everybody knows that it is the nature of every man to want to stick his cock inside every woman he sees and inseminate her. Queers violate that number one rule of nature. It's sick and it's an abomination."

Something about the word "inseminate" burrowed a hole into my skull and laid eggs there. I don't remember if I had ever wanted to stick my cock inside Anne, but after hearing "inseminate" drip from her lips like sour bile I never wanted to again. She may as well have grown a boil-and-tumor-ridden tentacle from her forehead for how unattractive I found her after that. *Inseminate. Inseminate. No, thank you all the same.*

BY THE TIME WE had gotten home most everyone was rowdy again, laughing and mocking the two queers with fairly spot-on impersonations of their cries for help and pity. Suzi chuckled a little bit. I guess I did too. Richard did not. Sherry seemed oblivious even then that anything had happened.

AS WE CLIMBED INTO bed Suzi said, "I don't feel like having sex tonight. But I'll suck on you if you need me to." "Suck on you" nestled into my brain real snug right next to "inseminate." It was a rather tight and uncomfortable fit. I kissed her quickly and silently and rolled over, bullshitting immediate slumber. Within a minute I heard her fall asleep for real. Girl could fall out on a dime. Must have been all the blows to the head.

I LAY THERE FOR close to an hour. My muscles twitched and throbbed, locking and unlocking, as the adrenaline drained from my system. I felt the familiar and inevitable emptiness that follows after a hard rush has faded. It's a hollow despair, entirely synthetic, only chemical.

AS I WALKED OUT to the kitchen I was bombarded with "OH RICHARD! FUCK ME PLEASE! HARDER! HARDER!!!" I ran to the bathroom and heaved into the toilet.

Rolling onto my back on the tiled floor I stared directly into the naked light bulb protruding from the ceiling. Shivering with cold muscle shakes. I felt gummy and white, like a chunk of beef jerky with the juices sucked out. Like a chlorinated open wound.

AFTER WHAT WAS CERTAINLY far too long to be lying on a bathroom floor, I stumbled back out into the kitchen. There I found Richard leaning against the sink downing a can of beer, doused in sweat, completely stark naked.

"Dude, my bad!" I said, retreating back into the bathroom.

"Hey Mikey," he said casually, "you have fun tonight?"

Whatever, I thought. If he wasn't bashful I figured there was no reason for me to be. *Well, I see what all the screaming is about anyway.*

"Yeah, sure," I said, coming out to the kitchen. He offered me a beer. I waved it off and he cracked it open and drank it himself.

"That's cool," he said. "Then maybe you can explain something to me. Beating up faggots. How exactly does that advance the revolution?" I didn't have an answer. He continued, "Are queers creating half-breeds? It seems to me that they are not. So how are they a problem? I mean, I don't really care one way or the other, but this isn't a game. I'm serious about this cause. Are we revolutionaries or thugs?"

"They spread fatal diseases," I offered.

"Good! I fucking applaud that! Look who's exterminated from that disease campaign. Niggers, drug addicts, the flab of the human race. I thought we were in favor of that sort of thing, or was there a meeting I wasn't invited to."

I should have seen this coming. Richard was known for his peculiar perspectives that occasionally flew in the face of the party line. His support for the state of Israel was the most egregious of these points. His devotion to the Republican Party was another sore spot, particularly as anti-government sentiment was on the rise within the movement. "This is no longer the party of Lincoln," he informed a group of bemused elders. "Hell, it's no longer the party of Goldwater or Nixon. You will alienate yourselves from this new rising power at your own peril, gentlemen." I often worried that this sort of thing would ultimately get us blackballed, but no one ever really debated Richard. They did grumble behind his back, old washwomen that they were.

"You said *campaign*," I told him. "Are you buying into the whole government plot theory?"

"This is all I'm saying," he replied. "Something that is destroying the scum of humanity is fine with me, whomever is responsible for unleashing it. Take that for what it's worth. Hell . . . I don't give a fuck. If you all get your jollies by beating down a bunch of sissies I'm not going to get in your way. Just don't lose sight of what really matters."

"I don't get it, Rich."

"What don't you get?"

"You love the fucking GOP but you hate the military worse than you hate fags."

"I don't love the GOP, first of all. I just recognize allies when I see them. And I don't hate the military either."

"But we're always fighting with soldiers. You're always calling them 'sheep.'"

"Tough love. I'm getting them strong for the real war."

"Ah . . ."

"And all those corporations that you loathe so much?"

"Yeah?"

"We're gonna take them over. We'll do the right thing for a change."

"Is that right?"

"Good night, Mikey. Stay focused. You're my man."

And that was that.

EIGHT

Extra credit. That was the only reason Sherry went to Brownard Auditorium that evening. Her Twentieth-Century American History prof was offering extra credit to anyone who attended the special "Civil Rights" hippity-dippity who-hah that evening, and given her less-than-stellar grades in that class, she needed all the bonus points she could scrounge up.

On the bill were a couple of old, local "freedom riders" there to regale the crowd with their harrowing tales of riding desegregated buses through the sixties South. Also on the program, a student was to be honored with a special award for outstanding-community-civil-rights-liberal-activist-whatever. I don't suppose I have to tell you who she was, do I?

Things briefly threatened to get interesting when a platoon of very frightening-looking uniformed black men entered the hall and stood in a solid line along the back wall. Apparently there was a black fraternity on campus that was kicked out some time in the late 1980s for some sort of overly militant activity. They re-formed off campus and remain a fearsome presence to this day, often showing up at open campus events. I believe they are called *Black United!* or *Black Unchained!* but I may have that all wrong. Their chapter head, or

Minister of Whitey Killin' or what have you, was none other than childhood chum of Jack Curry, Senbe Shabazz. By then their feud was in full swing. (Had they remained enemies . . . what would my life be like today? Perhaps it's best not to ponder that sort of thing.)

As soon as Niani and Jack and their rainbow coalition arrived there was immediate tension radiating from the back wall. Curry said something under his breath toward the perfect line of black power, baiting them in some fashion. Niani quickly grabbed him and dragged him away.

What the ancient bus people had to say was probably interesting, but they mumbled, and they were too quiet, and Sherry was bored and didn't really pay any attention. Few others did either, and the collective indifference toward these speakers apparently stuck in Ms. Shange's craw.

Some ridiculously overdressed black preacher served as master of ceremonies.

Now, don't get me wrong, Sherry said. *I had spent pretty much my entire life up until that point faithfully attending church every Sunday. I considered myself a fairly devout Christian lady. But try though I did, I could not understand half of what this fat, sweaty blowhard was yammering on about.*

Really it was just a grand show with a lot of histrionics and casting about, and most of what grunted through his lips was pure gibberish. ". . . and if we just put our faith in Jesus Christ, our Savior, we shall have no fear. Praise the Lord." The audience clapped and someone shouted *Amen!* and Sherry stared at her watch as the second hand clicked along. He continued, "I would like now to introduce to you all a most outstanding young lady. A woman whose tireless efforts, both on campus and in our community, have kept the work, the memory, and the spirit of the Reverend Doctor Martin Luther King Jr. alive for us today. Ladies and gentlemen, it is my honor and my privilege to present the Martin Luther King Christian Student Achievement Award to Miss Niani Shange."

The crowd applauded enthusiastically. Niani calmly stood and walked to the stage. People smiled warmly to her as she was handed her plaque. She took to the podium, smiling politely.

For a brief second, though, Sherry said, *I swear her eyes got all sharp and steely . . . and Jack-like . . .*

But then she softened again, smiling at the audience.

"Thank you, everyone," she said. "Thank you. And let me say what an honor it is for me to just hear my name mentioned in the same sentence as Dr. King's. And I am thrilled beyond words to be sharing the stage with all of these American heroes this evening." Polite applause from the peanut gallery. "I don't see courage like theirs much these days, and that's unfortunate, but we all benefit today from their sacrifice, and for that I thank them all. In keeping with the spirit of the evening, I hope you all would not mind indulging me for just a brief moment . . ."

Niani began to recite a poem from some old black writer Sherry had never heard of, *Count Somebody*, she thought, and neither was she terribly interested. Niani proceeded to talk about "Pagan hearts" and "shadowed places" and the like . . .

"'Not for myself I make this prayer . . .'" And so on, and so on, and so forth. Sherry went about absently doodling in her notebook. *This had better pay off*, Sherry thought.

But, at some point . . . Sherry couldn't help but sit up and take notice of the fact that the well-dressed Christians around her were not appreciating the performance all that much.

"'For me, my faith lies fallowing, I bow not 'til I see,'" Niani recited, then indicated with a sweep of her hand the audience before her, "'but *these* are humble and believe, bless their credulity . . .'"

A collective squirm began to resonate throughout the hall, and Niani went on. And on. There was no missing the murmur grumbling beneath the surface. She had their attention. No denying. And the vibe was getting ugly.

Sherry was not quite sure what all this talk about "black sheep" and "bastard kin" was about, but it seemed, as best as she could surmise, to be a fairly head-on "fuck you" to the crowd. *Why would she do this?* Sherry thought, torn halfway between sneaking out while the sneaking was still good . . . and wanting to see what might be going down. *Why is she trying to piss off the people that are here to honor her?* It just didn't make any sense. It reached a point where it didn't even matter what Niani was saying anymore. *It was how she said it.* Pointed at least. And incongruously venomous. *But still . . .*

Niani finally ended with an "Amen."

Nothing in return. "Amen?" she said again. One lone, nervous cough was heard from somewhere. "AMEN!" she shouted.

Dead silence. Long, agonizing, and thick as a cold fog. Niani looked out and smiled, oddly satisfied.

"In conclusion," she said after a while, "I would just like to say that it will be through perseverance and dedication, NOT blind faith and self-congratulatory complacency, that we will one day reach the promised land. The struggle continues. Thank you."

And with that she left the stage in silence. *Wow. What a bitch!* Sherry thought.

It was hard not to be intrigued, though.

As Niani walked toward the back of the hall there were a few scattered claps. Jack Curry met her in the middle aisle. He hugged her and they turned to leave. People rustled in their seats. A few got up to leave. The reverend rushed to the mic for a bit of spin control. "Thank you Miss Shange for that spirited . . . provocative . . . blah blah blah . . . genius of the Harlem Renaissance . . . vigilant and steadfast . . ." and so forth.

"*Assalaam-Alaikum,* Sister Niani," said Senbe Shabazz as Niani and Jack walked past.

"*Valaikum-Assalaam*, Brother Senbe," she replied politely.

"What, no 'ma lick'em' for me, Arnold?" Curry said, sour-faced, feigning hurt feelings.

"Hello, Mr. Curry," Shabazz said through his teeth.

"Goodbye, Mista Lincoln," said Jack with a dainty wave. (He even managed to make a sarcastic flip o' the wrist into something hideous and creepy.) And with that they left, leaving the Afro-militants behind. Shabazz tightened his lips in anger. The other men remained statues. Sherry exited quickly, not wanting any more to do with this situation. Credits be damned.

"Could you at least try to be civil sometimes?" Niani asked Jack as Sherry headed in the opposite direction.

To which he asked the posse, "Hey, do y'all think if he had read three books he'd have given himself three names?"

I HAD A FEELING *right then*, Sherry said, *that I would be getting to know that man very well very soon. He possessed what I wanted. What I couldn't live without.*

MEANWHILE, SUZI AND I had found ourselves in that corner of Relationshipville called "that odd place." Big surprise. Couples always talk about traveling through "that odd place." *We're going through that odd place right now.* And everyone nods knowingly, as if it weren't a completely pointless and ridiculous sojourn. Suzi would say she "wanted more" from our relationship, but would never tell me what that was. "If you don't know, I'm not going to tell you," she'd huff. Her shtick was to stay away for days at a time and not call. When I would do likewise she would break down and cry, "How can you just not call me?!?!" *I'm no good at mind games*, I'd tell her. *You win.* Occasionally she would accuse me of only wanting her around to fuck, which honestly was not true, but it's a hard charge to protest when you're a seventeen-year-old guy. That's just the way it is.

As a result I often had the joint to myself most of the evening when Richard was at the factory, which was a-okay with me. Despite repeated promises never to do so, we'd both started to entertain notions of attending college. Sherry had been on Richard about reenrolling for some time and it was beginning to take hold. "He's just so smart," she'd say. "I hate seeing him squander that. And you're smart too, Mikal." *For whatever that's worth.* So notions were at least wined and dined. Mine were fairly abstract, whereas Richard was really getting into the idea of exposing college professors for the Marxists he assumed they all were. When I mentioned that perhaps that was a flimsy reason to shell out such an obscene amount of money he replied, "I can't destroy and rebuild the system from the inside if I'm not inside. I've been to university before. It's not like it's difficult. I gotta get realistic if I'm gonna go big."

"How big are you planning to get?" I asked.

"All the way, my man. All the way. If that pants-shitting retard David Duke can make it, it'll be a cakewalk for me."

"What about all them tattoos you got? You're staring down the barrel of a helluvalotta laser work. How you gonna explain all that scar tissue to your potential constituency?"

"Two words: Agent Orange."

"You're going to lie about being in a war?"

"Oldest politico trick in the book."

"Nice."

I HAD FIGURED, WITH Richard slaving away on the assembly line until midnight, Sherry's post-class visits would cease. Or at least decrease. I figured wrong. Between Richard's late shift and Suzi's cold shoulder Sherry and I began spending more and more time together. Just the two of us. Another fairly odd place to be. It's hard to know how to feel.

At first I found her bothersome and obtrusive. Jabbery and self-absorbed and annoyingly insecure. Every day I'd dread the inevitable after-school special. The ritual was always the same. She'd come in, shed her books, her boots, her socks, march into the kitchen for a brew, come back in and plop onto the couch, and start in with, "What a day, I'll tell you what."

After a while, though, I began to expect her at a certain time, and I'd get irritable when she was late. As Richard's right-hand man, after all, I'd be derelict in my duties not to keep tabs on his prized possession, right? I started to worry about where she might be and whom she might be with. Instincts. Ignore them at your own peril.

Her story would usually involve some pompous, asshead prof, a lost loan payment, a combative classmate. But there was often some passing mention of "Curry and Shange and them," which would appear in the form of a single word: curryandshangeandthem, followed by pronounced rolling of the eyes. "I hear that Curry can speak five foreign languages . . . but the shit he says doesn't even make sense in English." "Shange is organizing a protest to counter-protest some other counter-protest that's protesting a protest nobody even knows about. Sheesh." As time went on, however, that seven-syllable word curryandshangeandthem morphed into a similar but significantly different one: jackandnianiandthem.

"Richard would want me keeping an eye on those people, don't you think Mikal? They're dangerous."

"Yeah . . ."

"I found out where they live at. The two of them anyway. Jamestown Street"

"It's pronounced *JAY-muss-ton*."

"You know where that is?"

"I'm familiar."

"Don't worry. I keep a safe distance. They don't even know I exist."

"I believe you." And I did. And I was wrong. Here's the lesson: never underestimate the all-seeing eye of the deranged paranoiac.

I wasn't sure what to do the day she came home teary and red-eyed, her face blotchy with salt burn. I still don't know what I should have done.

"Bad day?" I asked.

"Bad day," she replied.

"Okay . . . So . . . what happened?"

"Nothing much. I just get emotional sometimes."

"Hmmmm."

"Richard told me he loved me last night," she said with a sniffle. "I told him that I loved him too."

"Quit changing the subject. What happened today?"

"Jack Curry made me cry today. That's all." A poisonous chill ran through me. *Forever a specter* . . .

"Uh huh . . . Okay . . . Do you just want to not tell me, or are we playing a game here? I'm not into games, Sherry."

"Jack Curry grabbed me today and dragged me into a men's bathroom and slammed me against the wall and ripped my shirt open."

"WHAT?!?!?!?!?!"

"It's not as bad as it sounds."

"ARE YOU FUCKING CRAZY? Not as bad as it sounds?! We're gonna hunt that fucker down and destroy him!"

"NO! Don't do anything! Please, Mikal, please don't tell Richard!"

"Noooooooooooo dice. I HAVE to tell him. You know that."

"PLEASE! Just between us. He didn't hurt me, okay?"

"He dragged you into a fucking bathroom, threw you against a wall, and ripped your clothes off, and that's not hurting you?"

"You don't understand."

"He's DEAD. I understand that."

"No—"

"He's not going to see another morning."

"You tell Richard and I'll deny it. I'll tell him you've had a vendetta against the guy for years and now you're lying on me to get revenge. You wanna risk him taking my word over yours? You up for that challenge, Mikal?"

"WHY WOULD YOU DO THAT?!" I was beyond furious. At that point I didn't even care if Jack Curry had raped her. I didn't care if he had rammed his staff right up into her lungs. The fact that she would dare even think of driving a wedge between Richard and me . . .

"Why are you taking up for that fucking . . . swamp creature?" I demanded. "You fucking him?"

"NO!"

"You wanna fuck him?"

"Fuck you, Mikal! I'm with Richard only. I love Richard. And he loves me."

"You're playing with some serious shit, little girl. You just don't know."

"You're gonna make me cry too. Just like Jack. You both use your tongues like a weapon. You and Jack, you're just the same."

"Don't . . . you . . . EVER say that to me again, you rank little—"

"Listen to yourself, Mikal. Who do you sound like?"

"You don't know me."

"I do so know you. And I know him too."

"I'll bet you know him all right. I bet you let him nail you in that bathroom. I bet you yanked him off. I bet you licked it off his thigh."

"Keep talking, *Jack*. Same old song. The lyrics haven't changed."

"Get out of my house."

"You wanna throw me out? Huh? You wanna throw me

around? Wanna pin me to the wall? You wanna tear my clothes off?"

"Get the fucking hell out of my house."

"This is Richard's house."

"GET. OUT."

"Everybody pushes me away."

She stormed out. I sat there shaking with rage. Why? Why would she put me in that position? What really happened? I wanted her gone forever. I wished she had never come around. I knew I'd have to watch her now. For Richard. And I knew Richard couldn't know that I was watching her. I couldn't risk him knowing whatever she was up to. And I couldn't risk him knowing I was hiding things from him. I couldn't risk him suspecting me. I couldn't risk him pushing me away . . .

AN HOUR LATER, SHE called on the phone.

"I'm sorry."

"*I'm* sorry. Are you okay?"

"I'm okay. Still friends?"

"Still friends."

"Mikal?"

"Yeah?"

"How long do you think you're going to do this?"

"Do what?"

"Where do you see yourself in twenty-five years? Where do you see yourself in ten? Where do you see yourself in the future?"

"I don't."

"Hm. 'Kay. See ya."

And that was that.

NINE

Jack did not hurt me that day. Not physically. He hurt my feelings. Maybe I had that coming to me.

Sherry sat in the downstairs hallway alcove of the University Center right outside the bookstore. Watching them.

It was pretty boring, actually. They weren't really doing anything except goofing around by the greeting cards.

Sherry paged through the school newspaper a couple of times without really reading it. The front page contained a picture of Niani and a banner headline announcing: "Local Civic and Religious Leaders Outraged by Honored Student—'Out of Line,' Says Rev. Brinks." Sherry had the hall pretty much to herself, as it was noonish and most folks were in the cafeteria.

Out of line, she thought. *That's a good description of her across the board. Out of line. Out of order.*

Jack Curry and Niani exited the bookstore, bade each other a "see ya at home," and headed in opposite directions. Sherry stood up to go catch a bite when she felt a rough hand grab her collar and whip her around. Before she realized what happened she was trapped against the wall of the little boy's room. She tried to scream but couldn't even so much as squeak. Jack held her shoulders hard against the cold tile wall. She was paralyzed. His face mere inches from hers as he glared right into her. His eyes were like two pitch-black chasms. Nothing behind them.

"So howzaboutya, little ham?" he growled. "What's your story, THINK HARD NOW! Who are you and what the fuck do you want?"

She could barely eke out a sound.

"I . . . I . . . I—"

"Have been following us? Couldn't help but notice. Somebody send ya? Shit! Didn't think we were that important yet."

He squinted, noticing the top of her tattoo peeking out from under her blouse. He yanked the collar down and a button went flying, rolling across the floor and clinking into the corner. His face darkened further as he stared at the swastika, but he did not look surprised. *He's going to kill me.*

"For, for, for your information," she stuttered desperately, "that's a—"

"Sun wheel? Nice try, piglet. Pull the other one."

Right at that moment the door to the men's room flew open and some neckbone frat boy wandered in. He stopped short, staring at them. The three looked at each other in silence for a fat, stifled moment. Finally the guy just gave a little "my bad" salute, turned on his heel . . . and left.

As if suddenly realizing his trespass, Jack backed quickly away and walked to the opposite wall. Disgusted with himself. He turned his back, muttering, "Sorry. Sorry. Didn't mean it to be like that. That's not how I meant it. Not at all. No. No . . ."

If I ran, Sherry thought, *would he chase me? Should I say something?*

"Jack . . . look. I'm not trying to step on anybody's toes or anything."

"What?" he said turning toward her again. "What the hell are you talking about?"

I don't know.

"I'm not trying to get in the way, Jack. I just want to—"

"Huh? Jack? I've never even met you before! I don't fucking know your name."

I know.

"That girl," she stammered. "That black girl. Your girlfriend. See, I saw her . . . and maybe you don't know . . . I just really don't really think you know what I . . . or, what I mean is—"

"She's not my girlfriend," he said, his voice suddenly hollow. Distant.

"Oh . . . I see . . ."

Hmmmmm . . .

There was a long empty moment, then he turned his glare back on Sherry.

"You little Nazi spunk rag . . . Staking out a hit on her? Is that what's going on? Is that what you're doing? Little James Earl fuckin' Ray in a black lace bra? GODDAMN I thought you people were all gone by now!"

"IT'S NOT LIKE THAT!" Sherry screamed. Curry did not so much as blink. "I want to talk to you. Okay? Can we get out of this fucking toilet please?"

SO THEY WALKED IN silence.

I don't know where we were heading, we just strolled along the main lawn as if we had a purpose or destination.

Sherry caught the vibe that Jack Curry was barely tolerating her presence, and the slightest wrong move on her part would bring about dire consequences. So she kept her mouth shut. Across the way they saw Trey McKinley walking with Melanie. They called out to Jack and waved. He gave them the peace sign.

"What up, homey?" Trey yelled.

Painful.

"A'ight T-dog! A'ight Mel!" Jack replied, smiling . . . if you could call it that. Up close it was more like a wolf bearing fangs, but Sherry figured that's probably the best he could do.

Said Sherry, *I've always felt that a smile doesn't so much happen in the lips, it happens in the eyes. And looking at Jack just then I couldn't imagine those cold dead stones ever warming to even the tiniest smile.*

As Trey disappeared behind South Hall, Jack quietly sang the "witch's guard" melody from *The Wizard of Oz* . . .

"Oreo . . . reooooooooo . . ."

"Are you calling him an Oreo?" Sherry laughed.

"Not me," he said sarcastically. "That's not nice."

"If he's an Oreo, what are you?"

A thoughtful pause, then . . .

"Good question," he said nodding. "Naw, they're cool, though."

"I think he's a prick."

"He's okay."

Another pause.

"So . . . Jack, um, I hear that you're fluent in five different languages. Or is it six?"

"Eh, fluent is pushing it."

"It must be wild to be able to communicate with so many different people."

"Heh . . . yeah . . ."

Guy speaks five languages, Sherry thought, *but can only grunt at me.*

So they walked some more . . .

AND I BEGAN BLATHERING *on and on like an idiot. I don't even know how it started. Told him way too much. Where I was from, what my family was like, how hard it was to move away from home and my friends and my safe little cocoon, how Richard and I met. How welcome I felt in his circle of friends. (Shut up shut up!* I thought to myself. *Dumbass, shut up! But* nope, no such luck.) I didn't get into details about the Fifth Reich and pretty much shrugged off the whole "skinhead" thing as well as I could. I tried to make it sound like stupid little kid's stuff and not really a big deal at all. "It's just punk rock, you know? Pick your pose, get your costume together." I indicated his Napalm Death T-shirt. He didn't respond. I couldn't read him in the slightest. He didn't speak, and gave no indication that what I was saying meant anything to him. So I prattled on and on filling up the silence with whatever. Finally I cracked and started asking him questions head-on. How did he and his friends get together? How did they meet? What was his home life like? How long had he known Niani? Had they always been close? What made them tick, whirl, click, and whistle? What's it all about, Alfie? Nothing. He didn't answer me. At all. I finally gave up.

"I just want a little peek inside," I said, small. "That's all. What's your world like. There's something going on in there that's just so totally different and I just wanted to—"

"Uh huh," he said, stopping me short. "Okay. I'm gonna ask this in the nicest way I can think of . . . Are you really this fucking dense or is it an act?" I was stunned. He said it in such a casual way I had to hit a mental "rewind" to be sure I heard it right. He continued, "So, let's look at the play-by-play. You hooked up with a guy who bashes people's heads in cuz you thought he was ooooooo dangerous. A rebel. Leader of the pack. How exciting. But now . . . shucks, that's just not enough. Now you need some new honey pot to stick your fingers into. Fill that empty void. Is your life so bankrupt that you constantly need some new bullshit trial? Okay, and what could be more clandestine than for a skinhead's main squeeze to—"

"Look, asshole," I spat. "You don't have me figured out, okay? I'm not like that. I'm not looking to stick my fingers in any void. You fuck. I love my boyfriend and we've got our thing going and you've got yours." I should have stopped there. Alas, "I just thought maybe I could reach across the aisle and say 'hello,' but now I see you for what you are. Scared. You're too scared to *even talk to me." I don't know why, but I wanted to push him. I'd heard so much about how unhinged he was, I wanted to see how wide and hard I could make him swing. He tried to stare me down, and I would not flinch. And for a split second . . . I wondered if he thought I was pretty at all. "Left, right, it's all meaningless to me. Does it mean anything to you?" Nothing. "It's all about that girl," I continued. "You know it, I know it. That girl who's not your girl. The one that's so close . . . oh, but just out of reach. It's ALL about her. But . . . she's not with you. So why can't you let me in a little? You're never going to be happy like that anyway. "*

Oh my god, why did I say that? Like water on a grease fire—
"YOU DON'T KNOW A GODDAMN THING ABOUT FUCKALL, YOU INBRED COUNTRY-FRIED TWAT!!!"

"I've seen your type before. All your life you've walked in a haze with no thoughts of your own. Somebody else's fucking opinions, some pre-fab beliefs. A little sucking and squeezing in the back of a letterman's pickup or Pappy's outhouse and you think you know what's what. Now you're out in the 'real world' to find yourself and get your learn on but you're still too bottled-up Catholic, afraid God and your dead relatives are watching you masturbate. Can you hang with all the freakos and faggots and darkies running about? Wanna take a trip to the nigger side of town so long as you can go home after, right? What? Why you still here? What do you want from me? Go on, then! Run on back to your fucking boyfriend!"

"You're such a fucking jerk! People say, 'Oh, that's Jack. He looks like a monster, but he cares about folks.' But you don't care about anybody! You don't help anybody! You and your poseur bleeding-heart friends just put on a big show to impress fuckin'-everybody. But it's all BULLSHIT! You are just as cruel as anyone else, you hypocrite! Stop it. Shut up."

I started to cry. "I said stop it, you fucking bastard, I just wanted to talk. Fuck you! Can't we just talk?"

I was really bawling, and that just made him meaner.

"Oh is that what you are?! Is that where you live at?! SHUT UP! I'm leaving now, all right?! I'll leave you alone! I don't want anything from you! I don't want anything!!!"

HE SNARLED **BOYFRIEND** AND *began goose-stepping and throwing the salute. "Sieg heil! Sieg heil!" I covered my ears and ran away as fast as I could, sobbing, terrified and humiliated. "Run on home, Eva Braun!" he yelled. "Go on, Elly May Clampett, you hillbilly slut, go let your brothers gang fuck you some more! Run on back to the sticks, YOU FUCKING HICK!!!"*

SOME WOULD PROBABLY SAY *that that should have been enough to keep me away for good.*

But it wasn't.

TEN

Suzi called me around 9:30 PM. The waiting game was, apparently, over.

"You home alone?" she asked.

"Yep."

"Miss you."

"I'm always here. You can come over any time."

"How's about now?"

IT'S A PECULIAR THING, you know, how confident I was that everything between us would work out in the end. I was sure we'd weather any storm. Make it through the trials and tribulations. Uncertainly and strife, Mars and Venus, bend in the road's not the end of the road, all that dog shit. There was never a doubt in my mind. *Wait it out, it'll all be fine.* When I opened the door for her that night and she practically dove into my arms I thought to myself, *Nicely played, old chap. Jolly good show indeed.*

WITHOUT A WORD SPOKEN we rushed to my room on the back porch, freed each other of any and all burdensome clothing, and fell in a naked heap onto my futon, gobbling each other alive.

"Wait!" she gasped. "Do y-you . . . really want to . . . really t-take me there?"

"Yes! Of course! Anything you want!"

"Go g- . . . get ice."

I ran out to the kitchen and yanked an ice tray out of the freezer that had frozen, frost covered, onto the door. Contained therein was exactly one cube. When I got back to the porch she had already started without me, working her fingertips between her thighs, curling her wrist in circles. "Round off the edges for me," she whispered biting her lip, her eyes shut tight. I put the cube in my mouth, twisting it back and forth in my lips, melting it into a workable dome shape. From there I simply did as I was told, following her every instruction to the letter. "Rub it here . . . Oh yes, that's it, right there . . . Slide it back in . . . deeper. Just like that, in a circle . . . oh god yes, right like that . . ." She shuddered and squirmed, her arms locked stiff as she grabbed hold of the sheets with both hands. Her moaning got louder as her breaths shortened, her head jerking back and forth across the cushion. "Oh god, Mikal, I don't know . . . if I c-cuh-can taaaaaaake . . . much more!" All at once she arched her back, bucking hard against my hand. She screamed, thrashing up and down on the mattress as I felt the diminishing ice cube disappear into oblivion. She rolled away from me, curling up into a ball at the top right corner of the futon, shivering and cooing. "Oh fuck . . . Oh Jesus . . . That was amaaaaaazing . . . Ooooooooo my god, it's shooting all through my body. Little micro-gasms all over. I can feel it in my toes!" I sat back beaming, feeling fifteen feet tall and cast-iron. I don't know how much I could honestly have taken credit for, but I was proud to be a part of it at any rate. "Oh fuck yeah . . ." she continued, panting, wiping a tear from her cheek. "That's it right there. That's just how

HE does it. Yeah. That's what he does to me. And she's so jealous. She's jealous of me."

I sat granite still, dumbstruck, my mouth gaping open like a mounted trout. She didn't even notice.

"Oh yeah," she said. "She is so jealous of what we share."

AND THAT'S HOW SHE opted to tell me.

BUT LET'S BE HONEST, I kind of already knew, didn't I?

ELEVEN

Not many people know about my brother. Kaleb was his name. Two years my junior. I barely remember him. Died when I was eight. I've since met a number of people who have survived leukemia, but when Kaleb was diagnosed I don't remember death being anything but a forgone conclusion. He fought like a champ, you know. But he was just so goddamn little. My people are slight folk as a rule on both Mom's and Dad's sides, and he was tiny even by our standards. I don't even remember going to his funeral. Perhaps I didn't go.

WE WERE STILL LIVING in Louisville, I was ten or eleven, the first time I ever stood up to my father. I don't recall what set him off, but he was whaling on Mom with a curtain rod. She shrieked and blubbered, curled up on the kitchen floor, and I ran in and jumped between them. Dad didn't so much as pause, he simply kept whacking—on me instead—as I was in the way.

"Get the fuck out, Mikal, or I'll beat yer ass bloody!"

I didn't flinch, though it stung like a thousand hornets. I called him a "weak asshole" and told him if he touched my mother again I'd slit his throat while he slept. "Don't sleep, you weak asshole," I said, short on words just then. He called me "tough guy" and pulled out his .357. Of course it was loaded. It always was and so was he. My mother crawled up on her knees and threw her arms around me, sobbing, begging him to put it away.

"Ya heard 'im threaten me, Tanya!" he yelled, waving the gun back and forth between my mother and me. He stumbled a bit in a deep vodka drunk and cocked the piece. My arms and neck throbbed. The bass drum in my ear needed tuning.

All at once he fell to the floor in a weeping heap. He dropped the gun under the table and I had a mind to grab it and shoot his face clean off.

"I love y'all so much," he cried. "I'm so sorry!" He began cradling his arm, rocking back and forth, snot, tears, and drool spilling down his face. "My baby boy," he sobbed into the negative space in the crook of his arm where a baby would be. "My baby K . . . where's my baby K at . . . where's he at . . ."

"You let him die," I said. "He could have lived, but you let him die."

"Where's he at, my tiny little baby boy . . ."

I spat on him and called him out for a "queer." Mom grabbed me and we ran out of the house. Nowhere else to go, we stayed in a gnarly-ass roach motel called The Pit Stop Lodge.

She called him that night. Of course. He pleaded with her to come home. He promised he'd never hurt her or me again, and he swore he'd never pull the gun on us ever again, and he vowed on his mother's eternal grave to get rid of the gun once and for all. But he did, and he did, and he didn't. That's just the way it is.

"SUZI, THIS HAS TO stop right now!"

I paced about in a frothing rage, flinging my arms aimlessly about as she, cool and calm, got dressed and prepared to leave.

"You just don't understand, Mikal. You don't understand the bond that we have, him and me. The love that's between us. I'm sorry. I never wanted to hurt you."

"Hurt ME?! I ain't the one who's fucking HURT, Suze! We got to go to the cops! We can't let that diseased bastard get away with this!"

"Don't you talk about Daddy like that!"

"How can you call that fucking cretin 'Daddy'?! This is the most morally di—"

"Ooooooooooh morals." She threw up her hands in a grand display. "That means a FAT lot coming from you, Mikal. Mister Aryan Nation. How many times have I watched you attack people—who never done a thing to you—and beat them half to death? Huh? How many times? How many people have you hurt? Not for your so-called 'revolution,' but just because it got your rocks off. And you want to lecture me about morals? You've got balls, my love. Big, heavy, metal balls swinging right between your knees. Morals. Ho ho ho. Too funny for words."

"You want me to quit, Suzi? Do you? Cuz I will. If it bothers you, then I promise on my life that I won't never harm another person so long as I live, no matter what. Okay? I'll give it ALL up if that's what you want. All of this. Okay?! I would do that *for you*." And I meant it.

"No, I don't think you will, Mikal. And for the record, I don't care what you do and I don't care who you stomp. Some people are sub-human and they get what they deserve. But that's beside the point. I don't think you ever would quit, no matter what you say. It's not because I don't think you're sincere. It's because I know in my heart that I'm not your first love." She indicated Richard's bedroom door. My face burned so hot you could have lit kindling off my forehead. I wanted to grab her and slap her hard for crossing that line. I wanted to scream at her and shake some sense into her. But I simply stood rigid, and with all my strength forced a meager smile.

"Yeah, Suze? Well . . . I know I ain't your first love neither."

"You're damn right you're not." And she walked out. And that was that.

I never saw her again.

I DIDN'T TELL ANYONE why Suzi and I had broken up. "It just happens, you know. People grow apart." I figured they would find out on their own someday anyway. I was right. But that next night it was all about Cheer Mikey Up, so we hit the town running, everyone promising to buy me a drink. A promise they all made good on, though I now certainly wish that they hadn't.

YEAH, WE PAINTED THE town red, all right. And we had help. At about 1:30 AM, after hitting every bar that would let us in, we headed across the viaduct to the West Side. See what was shaking at that guy Meat's place. We never made it that far.

I STILL DON'T KNOW where exactly we were, but I was the first to spot them.

"Hey, Sssshurry," I slurred, pointing out the window as we stopped for a red light, "ain't that that nigger you wanted us we should stomp up the uth'r night at Lucree . . . sha's . . . ?"

"Yup," she said. "That's old Oreo Trey and his white chocolate arm candy Melanie."

With that, Joe threw the van in reverse, slammed it in drive, and peeled up to the sidewalk.

"I think these number ones need a lesson," Joe announced. "Do I hear a 'nay'?"

With that everyone poured out of the van. Upon seeing us, Trey and Melanie froze in terror. I don't think anyone spoke. There was no pause or hesitation. We all just immediately lunged for the guy. We beat him to the ground and went in for a circle kick. Melanie ran off screaming and Richard yelled at the girls, "FUCKING GET HER!"

SHERRY SAID:

Little girl was quick. Must have been an athlete or something. She kicked off her high heels and was definitely faster barefoot than we were in those big, clompy boots. At some point she was so far ahead of us she was completely out of sight. By the time we caught up to her she had wedged herself L-shape into a phone booth, already talking frantically to someone. It suddenly occurred to me that this chick could identify me. Plus I'd have to see them at school Monday, or eventually anyway. So I stayed back as Anne, Jennie, and Reeba all went flying at the booth.

"Get out of there, bitch!" one of them screamed at her. The three kicked furiously at the Plexiglas booth, successfully breaking in one side. Melanie cried and wailed, pressing her bare feet against the glass to keep them out.

"Hurry, please!" I heard her sob into the receiver. The scene was starting to attract attention from the locals, so we darted off.

"I UNDERSTAND THE BIND you're in, fella," Richard said to Trey McKinley, who was barely conscious. Trey attempted to speak, but only succeeded in creating a low gurgle, and tiny bubbles of blood. His face was beaten so out of shape he barely looked like the same man. The smell of blood collided with the copious amount of alcohol sloshing about in my stomach and I began to feel dizzy and sick. "I mean," Richard continued, laying on his fake *I'm reasonable* routine, "black women are some surly, ugly, nasty bitches. I know that. I see 'em flashing their shit on the street corners downtown. 'Hoes' you call 'em? No doubt. But that simply does not give

you the right to pump your filthy seed inside *our* women.
Are you straight hip to my lingo, brutha?"

"Ha ha, yeah," Brian snorted. "Are we down, homey?"

DUTY DONE, WE WERE about to leave him there sleeping on the curb and go find the girls, when suddenly this
huge brown Cadillac screeched to a halt right next to us. Out
stepped Jack Curry, this young Japanese headbanger I later
found out was named Yoshimoto, and six of the biggest, dark-
est, hardest homeboys who ever lived. These guys had a good
ten years on us, probably hard time, and countless pounds of
muscle. *Oh fuck fuck fuck . . . Blackchurch . . . represent . . .*

"Just hang tight, lil cuz," one of them said to Trey, who
likely did not hear him. They all began to circle us. My head
was spinning and I stumbled, like I had just stepped onto a
moving carousel (a feeling to which I have grown quite ac-
customed).

"All right then, T," said Yoshimoto. Some wet mumble
burbled from the sidewalk.

"Don't worry, Trey," said Curry. "We'll have you up on two
and voting Republican again in no time."

We were completely walled in. No escape, but it did occur
to me, even in my drunken state, that in that formation they
likely didn't have guns. I'll take my pluses where I can get
them. I heard a click that I knew was Richard's switchblade.

"Okay," Richard yawned, "let's get this over with."

To this day I don't know what he was thinking. There was
no way we could take these guys and no way out. Did he
miscalculate? Had his head gotten too big? They came down
on us like collapsing walls. I barely got one swing in when I
felt a wrecking ball slam into my stomach from two coun-
ties over. I hit the pavement knees first, spilling a river of
blood and booze vomit out into the street. I felt a boot heel
jam into my kidneys and another crack the back of my skull

as I flew cheek-first into a rusty wheel well. A slam to the chest and two pops to the face and that was it for me. There was a lot of "Whatchoo thought, fool!" and "Betta reckonize, punk!" kind of chatter. *Feels like home, by gum.* I crawled up to the sidewalk to see someone scoop up Trey and carry him to the Caddie, which proceeded to squeal off into the night. My boys held their own, more or less, but it was the most brutal beat-down any of us had ever caught. I appeared to have been deemed either out of commission or no longer present as I lay there watching through blurry, swelling eyes. Closest to me Curry and Phil were doing a number on each other, Phil managing a solid whack to Curry's shoulder with a thick metal chain. In a flash Curry got the upper hand and slammed Phil's face into the bumper of the parked car. From there he brought his boots down on Phil's wrists, one then the other, the second *smash* even more devastating than the first. Phil shrieked in agony. He continued to howl as Curry dragged him into an adjacent alleyway. From there all I heard was the occasional dull grunt and the moist pounding of beef being tenderized.

Sirens began to wail in the distance. Rapidly approaching. All present tore off into the night every which way. Except for me, of course, and whatever unspeakable horror was taking place in the alley. I attempted to stand, and fell immediately again onto the sidewalk. I tried to speak and hacked up more blood instead.

SHERRY SAID:

The girls and I panicked when we heard the sirens. We freaked when we saw the rollers speed past, heading in the direction of where we had left you boys. We went to hide out at a nearby gas station and screamed at each for a half an hour about what to do. Finally Reeba called her brother Kevin and he came to pick us up. We were too afraid to go back to Richard's place so we ended up staying at Kevin's house on the West Side until about five or six AM. *I called and left a message for Richard telling him where we were and to please call or come over as soon as he could.*

The rest of the girls fell asleep after a while, but I couldn't, so I sat in the kitchen all by myself. At some point Kevin came in. He was nice at first, asking me if I was okay and if I needed anything. He handed me a beer from the fridge and asked if I was hungry. Then he asked me if I felt grateful . . . and in a flash I wanted to run. I didn't say a word.

"Don't look so freaked, pretty girl," he said, lighting a cigarette. "Yer safe now. "

"I'm just a little . . . shook up."

"That'll teach ya not to play where you oughtn't."

He came right out with it that he would really like to butt-fuck me and I should let him because if it hadn't been for him, "the niggers would be sucking the meat off your bones right now." He pulled his penis out of his sweatshorts and presented it to me like an offering. It was half-hard and hung crooked. I gave it a few awkward pulls and felt it stiffen in my fingers. I started to cry. He snorted in disgust, stuffed it back into his pants, and shuffled off back to bed. I made a mental note to tell Richard about it later and have him settle that piece of shit but good. I never cashed in on it. Call it a lost opportunity.

Desperate for some shut-eye, I went out to the living room and scooted Anne over so I could grab a bit of couch space. She rested her head on my shoulder and cuddled against me, never waking. I closed my eyes and pretended she was someone else.

WHEN I HEARD LATER *how things had gone down and what Jack had done to Phil, I wasn't surprised. And it was hard to know how to feel.*

———————

I HADN'T FELT IT at first, but the jagged corner of the wheel well had lacerated my cheek, and it throbbed and pounded as I crawled slowly on my elbows toward the alley. I saw Jack Curry prop Phil into a sitting position and kneel before him face-to-face. Phil tried desperately to punch him, but his crushed wrists made it a futile effort.

"I am so happy for you, man," I heard Curry say, his voice hideously giddy. "You must be so excited!" The sirens grew ever closer. I dragged myself up and fell against the brick wall. "You're gonna love this, dude," Curry said like a sugared-up ten-year-old. "Scout's honor."

I saw his hand slide into Phil's front pants pocket. Rooted about for a moment, then pulled out Phil's brass knuckles. I tried to yell, but I still had no wind in my lungs and retched up a thin string of blood instead. I lunged forward and hit the pavement once again. *Pathetic. Pathetic!* Curry did not notice, or didn't bother to care, but Phil saw me. Our eyes met, and I'd never seen him so terrified. I'd never seen *anyone* so terrified. Even those two queers we stomped in Candyland weren't as afraid of us as Phil was of Jack Curry just then. And with good cause. Those queers likely recovered in a couple of weeks. No such luck for Phil.

"No!" Phil begged "Please! Please don't!"

Curry just laughed.

"Love it! You'll love it. Trust me. Don't worry. I'm a man of peace."

SMAAAAAASH!!! The sound of a brass-knuckled hook punch square into Phil's mouth. The echo of his jaw shattering bounced from building to building, reflecting all throughout the streets. Gushes of blood and fragments of broken molars spilled from Phil's open mouth as he gurgled in incoherent misery.

"Awwww . . . fuuuuuuuuugggggggg . . ."

Curry proceeded to slam him twice more in his already pulverized jaw. Just then two squad cars barreled in, blocking

the street both ways. Curry picked up Phil and tossed him
out into the road, then darted the opposite way down the
alley. I closed my eyes and they fused shut.

"JESUS, BOY," I HEARD a voice say. I didn't know if it
was directed toward me or not. "Can you talk?" Phil's ability
to speak, or lack thereof, should have been obvious, so I proceeded to tell the disembodied cop voice,

"We was jumped. Big gang of blacks. A drug gang I bet."

"You have any drugs on you now, son?"

"Oh NO, sir. Never."

It was true. No weapons either at the moment. I'll take my
pluses where I can get them.

PHIL WAS RUSHED TO Mercy Hospital (and so had been
Trey McKinley). I was taken to the police station and given an
obscene amount of ancient, tar-thick coffee. After I became
more lucid I gave the police my report. Seems my friend and
I had been driving home from a party when we were car-
jacked by a gang of thugs. The leader had a mouthful of gold
teeth and said something about payback for Rodney King.
Then they beat us up and stole my 92 CRX hatchback, which
my friend had been driving for me. And that's exactly how it
was, officers, I swear to The Good Lord Above.

"Well, what did y'all expect driving through that neighborhood?" a cop scolded. "You boys should have more sense
when it comes to those people." They bought it. Cops always
buy that story. Try it, you'll see.

"Believe me, sir," I said, laying it on, "we tried to get
through there as quick as all git-out, but the car ahead of us
stopped to talk to another driver coming the other way. They
was blocking traffic both ways! We was sitting ducks."

"That sounds about right," the officer said, nodding. Hook. Line. Sinker. Almost too easy.

They decided that, although I'd probably be pissing blood for a couple of days, my injuries were relatively minor, provided my tetanus shots were up to date (not likely). I did get a stern lecture about being an underage drunk. "Son, you're playing a loser game here." Thinking they were really giving it to me tough they threatened to call my folks, then proceeded to do just that. I pretended to be all worried and scared straight. It was hard not to laugh when the officer who called my parents came back looking vexed and perplexed.

"I . . . don't . . . think . . . your father is in any . . . condition to drive."

I offered to call "my brother" to come pick me up.

RICHARD ARRIVED AT THE station wearing a baseball cap and varsity football jacket from some school I'd never heard of. I suppose that was his stab at looking like a "regular guy." He yelled at me in front of everybody about being intoxicated, then said we had to "pray extra hard at church tomorrow." It was simultaneously overdone *and* half-baked, but the boys in blue ate it up.

ALL JOKING AROUND HAD blown away on the early-morning breeze by the time we got out to the van, however. The rest of the guys sat there huddled down, beaten to shit, bashed, and bandaged up.

"Well . . . that went good, huh?"

"We didn't want to leave y'all, Mikey," Brian said.

"It's all right. You did what you had to."

"Fucking niggers," said Geoff.

"They did what they had to," Richard replied.

WE DIDN'T SPEAK AGAIN until we pulled up outside Reeba's brother's house to collect the girls.

"From now on," Richard said in full boss voice, "no one leaves the house without a pistol." He looked right at me as if I had done something wrong. "No one."

AS SHOTGUN IT WAS my job to run up to the house and do the collecting. Reeba's brother Kevin answered the door. Seemed like a nice enough guy.

As we slid the van door open to let the girls in, Reeba instantly noticed Phil's absence and fell into screaming hysterics. I wanted to slap her.

Shut up, cunt. Nobody asked for your input.

TWELVE

It was a long night. Sherry was exhausted. She felt grimy and sick. It was close to 8:30 AM when they entered Mercy Hospital. They were told Phil would get into surgery as soon as possible, but there was no point in waiting around.

Richard dropped Sherry off at her dorm and they made plans to go see Phil later.

HAD SHE NOT BEEN so exhausted Sherry would have laughed out loud when her roommate Sarah laid eyes on her. It hadn't occurred to Sherry until just then, but this was the first time they had been in contact since her "makeover."

"Sharon?" Sarah asked blinking.

"It's hell out there kid," Sherry replied, rehanging her giant poster of Norma Jean that had obviously been ripped down. "I'm going to sleep for long, long time. You wake me up and I'll suck your eyeballs out of your goddamn skull."

RICHARD, REEBA, AND BRIAN came to pick Sherry up around 7:45 PM. It was after visiting hours, but Richard had worked something out so that they could see Phil. It was hard not to notice that Reeba had already begun the process of "unloading Phil," and Brian was perfectly willing to fill that vacant hole.

"Don't worry, Phil," Richard said. "We'll find the cock-sucker who did this. He'll be maggot breakfast by end of the week."

Phil lay in bed with both his arms elevated and his swollen jaw bandaged and wired shut. I'd been at the hospital all day. Promised I'd stay by him. I don't know why exactly. I felt that I owed it to him.

"Shorget adout it, Rish. Goezh wit ta territory."

He looked deformed. Misshapen. His left eye was swollen closed. But the worst bit of it, and he knew it, we all knew it, was that he was *different* from us now. He didn't look like us anymore. He couldn't do what we could do. He was no lon-ger a soldier. He was a cripple. Even in the world of low-rent fascism, there's nothing lower than the cripple.

He looked up at Reeba with his one working eye. She ran her fingers lightly over his ravaged, broken face. He knew she wasn't his anymore. Brian would fuck her and that would be that. He'd never have her again. And he'd have to choose be-tween sitting around eating through a straw, with his hands so bound and bandaged he can't even jerk off, while the woman he loves is gobbling his friend's cock in the next room . . . or he could leave for good and be completely on his own. Tough call.

After a while, whatever Richard, Brian, and Reeba had to say to Phil became nothing but low static to me. Sherry and I stared silently at one another. Pretended we weren't. It was ridiculous, but we shared a secret. *A stupid, pointless secret we shouldn't be keeping. Tell them, or I will. Tell them, or I will. But I didn't.*

WHEN IT WAS TIME for everyone to leave I walked down to the lobby with them. Richard said he would come pick me up in the morning. I said okay, although I planned to be alone the next day and would just as soon take the Metro. Whatever.

HEADING BACK TO PHIL'S room I stopped in the men's room, sweating and anxious. Anyone who can watch a stream of blood spray out from the end of his dick and not want to take his own life right then and there is a stronger man than I. As I steadied my left hand against the wall and prepared for the searing gasoline burn of another red piss I wondered how many blows to the kidney I had delivered in the past couple of months. Twelve? Fifteen? More? I tried not to think about it. *Fuck it! That's just the way it is! You take it as it comes.* The second an Aryan Warrior starts sweating about karma is the moment he may as well cash it all in for tie-dye and some groovy crystals.

AS I WALKED DOWN the hall toward Phil's room I heard him trying to yell at someone. I ran in just in time to hear, "What shou want? Tanks?! I owe 'ou shit, houshe nanny!" And catch Niani Shange walking out. *What the hell?*

"Excuse me," she said as she squeezed past me out into the hallway. I didn't breathe. I shut my eyes. Even for such a brief moment, it was surreal being that close to her. *Be gone.*

"Dring ne ny dinner too, cunt!!!" Phil hollered.

I walked into the room to see a milkshake sitting on his tray table.

"Strawberry?" I asked. He turned his head away from me. And then she spoke . . .

"Mikal? Mikal Fanon, is that you?"

I spun around to see her standing in the doorway. My mouth went completely dry and I felt like I would choke if I tried to swallow. She looked right at me. Right into my eyes. "Mikal Fanon. It is you, isn't it. I remember you from the old neighborhood. How are you? It's been a long time. Couple years anyway." I was stone-cold silent, staring at her like a feeb. "Do you remember me? I lived in the house three down from you. On the left." Nothing. "What have you been up to?" I opened my mouth but there was no sound. *Talk! Speak! Grunt! Gesticulate! Something!!!* "Do you remember my brother 'Zekial?" *FUCKING RETARD!* "How are your folks? How is your dad's hand? Is he better?"

Nothing.

I . . . got . . . nothing. I got nothing for you . . .

Finally she just nodded. "Okay," she said.

And she walked away.

I WENT AND SAT down in the chair next to Phil's bed. Not a word. Still. He made no indication that he wanted a drink of the shake. It just sat there. With my throat hot and dry like the goddamn Mojave I had half a mind to just grab it and slurp it all down. But I didn't. So we sat there in silence as the shake melted. Then it got warm and spoiled.

I TURNED ON THE TV and it all sucked. I turned it off again. I was just about to curl up in the chair and try to get some sleep when the last visitor of the night crawled out of the hottest pit in Hell and popped by for a "sweet dreams."

Upon seeing Jack Curry, Phil panicked and went to reach for the nurse call button, which was attached to a cord by his right hand. Jack grabbed it and stopped him flat.

"Hey hey hey. No need for that now, buddy."

"Whak ta fuck do zhou wonk?"

"Just stopping by to see how you're doing. That's all."

I wished I had a knife. For just a moment . . . I wished I had a gun.

"Dey hat ta show ny fuckin zhaw shuk!"

"Sewed your jaw shut, huh. That's a pisser."

I stood up and was about to lunge at Curry when he said, cold as a reptile, "Sit back down or I'll slash your throat all the way open. Go ahead and test me." He didn't even look my way. I doubt he even saw me out of the corner of his eye. He just sensed me. I didn't sit, but I stood paralyzed. Paralyzed and mute. *And stupid. And worthless.*

"GET TA FUCK ARAY FRON NE!!!"

Curry put his hand over Phil's mouth. Phil thrashed and shrieked in agony from the pressure.

"If you settle down, I'll take my hand away."

Phil tried to calm himself as tears began to stream down his face. I couldn't move. *I'm a lifeless fucking husk.* I wished I was dead.

"You know . . . Philip, is it? You know, Philip, I understand the bind you're in. I mean, shit! You're white! You should be running the damn show, correct? Your ancestors kicked ass. Massacred, enslaved, and infected everybody. So why aren't you calling any shots. Poor? Ignorant? No education? Couldn't keep a decent job even if you could get one, right? God. It's just so unfair. And the minorities get everything handed to them on a silver fucking platter, don't they. I feel for you, my strong white brother. I really do."

"Shou're a got tan rayshe traitor," Phil hissed.

Curry laughed.

"Race traitor? Did you say 'race traitor,' Philip? Do people even still say that? Guess you do." He slapped Phil in the jaw. Phil winced and shook off the pain, trying to stifle the scream welling up. I looked about the room for something to smash over Curry's head. "I'm sorry. Shouldn't have done that. I'll make it better." He bent over and licked a teardrop that was streaming down Phil's cheek. Just at that moment, a nurse walked in . . . froze in her tracks . . . giggled . . . gave a little "my bad" salute . . . and walked away. And Jack Curry laughed and laughed. And Phil shook with rage. And I wished I was dead.

"I'll be seeing you guys," he chuckled. "Stay strong. The white race needs men like you." And he was gone.

You're fucking worthless, I thought to myself. *Goddamn fucking worthless.*

"What tah fuck, Nikal," Phil said softly, sniffling.

"I'll kill him for you, Phil. I promise. I will kill him."

IT WAS LATE. MIDNIGHT maybe. Maybe one. Hospitals at midnight are like sterile catacombs, but without the comfort of knowing the worst is over. I went for another fire piss. Not as horrible that time. *Let the healing begin.*

I didn't want to go looking for Trey McKinley's room. But I knew I would. Autopilot took me there.

I stood in the doorway watching him sleep. His neck was braced and his face was bruised, both eyes puffy and knotted. But he didn't look too bad. It certainly wasn't his best day, but he didn't look all that bad. And he appeared to sleep in relative comfort. Cards and flowers all about the room. Already. An empty milkshake cup in the trash.

"I ain't sorry," I growled under my breath. "You got what you deserved. You hear me, nigger? I said, I ain't sorry."

"I hear you," he said without opening his eyes. And I wished I was dead.

THIRTEEN

The phone rang at about 11:30 AM. To say the very least, I was not entirely awake.

"Helluh? I'm lookin' fer Mikal Fanon."

"You found him."

"Dude!"

"Holy shit! How you been, man? You still living in Louisville?"

"Yep 'er. Can't complain too much. I've had a bitch of a time tracking you down, hoss."

"Yeah, I'm off the radar these days."

"Chup to?"

"Nothin' really."

"School or anything?"

"I'm a Fifth Reich Skin."

"A who?"

"Yeah."

"Is . . . that what, like a gang?"

"Yeah . . . sorta . . ."

"Like the Crips?"

"Yeah . . . well, no . . . kind of . . ."

I don't know how long we talked. Maybe an hour. I kept

falling asleep. He was working in his dad's auto shop. He got married, had a son, all that dull shit.

"Hey Mikey, you remember that guy I had to . . . you know, the guy I had to shoot?"

"Uh huh."

"I got ahold of his autopsy photos. You wanna see 'um?"

We made plans to get together. I never followed through. I try to make it a point to leave the past in the past. When possible. Talking to him, I walked past the bathroom and looked in the mirror at myself. *This isn't even the guy he knows*, I thought. *So long, bud. Best of luck to you.*

THE ANGRY GASH IN my left cheek kept me from shaving, which yielded a thoroughly unimpressive teenage beard. It was enough for Richard to start calling me "Jerry Garcia," however. I actually earned a string of nicknames at that time. Although I was no longer shaving my face, I was still shaving my head, which was not a good look at all, so I had taken to wearing a knit skullcap. And so I became "Johnny Grunge," "Mikal-in-Chains," and one of Sherry's invention, "Mudhoney," which everyone thought was hilarious but only Richard understood. Because of said misunderstanding I also ended up as "Mud Pony," "Mud Bunny," and often just "Mud." I was a good sport about it, though, and danced about singing the song "My Name Is Mud," which also no one got. Good times.

THE FIRST WEEK AFTER the downfall of Phil was fairly rough for me as Brian and Reeba had taken to spending all afternoon in the abandoned apartment next door rutting and caterwauling like feral felines.

"Goddamn," Reeba said to me passing through to get to the fridge. "I never knew it could be that good."

"Your thighs are bruised up."

"Why you lookin' at my thighs, Mikal-in-Chains?"

As I would sit there turning up the TV or the stereo as loudly as I could the thought crossed my mind that perhaps having to listen to other people fuck is my lot in life, my destiny, and maybe it's punishment for some wrongdoing from a past existence. I also wondered if that thought had ever occurred to Suzi's mother.

The heavens did smile upon me after that first week, however. Reeba's brother Kevin and his wife and two daughters had decided to take an extended trip down to Huntsville, Alabama, to stay with some great-grandaunt who was dying of throat cancer. So Reeba and Brian moved in over at their house to keep an eye on things.

I GOT TO ENJOY being home alone more and more, and I found that the time spent completely by myself was by far my happiest. Richard and I, by that time, had become something of a crotchety old couple, not really speaking around the house except to bitch about there being no food or the place being a mess. I'll admit that I've never been much of a housekeeper, but I usually kept the kitchen pretty well stocked. We lived right behind an IGA and I'm a fairly skilled thief. It's a talent, not a gift. It pissed me off when he griped about the food situation because I did my best to make sure we always had his favorite things, even at the expense of my own preferences. And it was my ass risking arrest every time I went "shopping." But it was never good enough for him.

I was rummaging through Richard's room one day looking for the phone when I discovered his chest o' weapons. He kept everything in fairly neat order: knives in sheaths, firearms in shoeboxes. I pulled out his nine and inspected it top to bottom. You always hear how heavy those things are, but you really don't think about it until it's in your hand. Richard's was perfectly polished, of course, oiled, and well maintained. And loaded. I flipped the safety off, slid the long barrel into my mouth, and pressed the muzzle to the back of my throat. It clicked against my incisors, which almost made me bite down reflexively. I cocked the hammer back and shut my eyes tightly, trying not to gag, rubbing my index finger against the trigger. Just then I heard the front door slam.

"Mikal?"

"I'm in here, Sherry."

"Can I come in?"

"No. I'm sleeping." I put the gun back in the box and closed the chest.

"Are you naked?"

"What?"

"I'm tired too. Can I go sleep in your bed?"

"Knock yourself out."

I CAME OUT TO the living room and found her usual heap of stuff by the door. Why I decided that day to look through her book bag I don't know. But I did. That's just the way it was. Usual stuff: textbooks, floppy discs, crumpled-up papers. There was also a small plastic bag of weed. *Huh* . . . I unrolled it to take a sniff, then closed it back up again. I didn't want to get a contact buzz. I also found a flyer for a party that Friday night. An "all-campus block rocker." "Come one come all." On Jamestown Street.

I went out to my room and found her sleeping on my futon in nothing but panties and a white T-shirt. Her dark black swastika tattoo screamed through the thin cotton.

"Uh," I said. "I'm up now, so you can go to Richard's room if you want. Probably more comfortable."

"Okaaaay," she mewed, not opening her eyes. She rolled over and wrapped her thighs around a pillow. "Your bed is gross." But she made no move to get up. "Will you cover my feet up, Mikal? They're freezing."

I covered her with a quilt and turned to leave.

"Oh, hey," I said. "I don't know if you know, but there's a big party at Meat's on Friday. Kind of a 'Get Better, Phil' thing."

"Sounds fun, but I gotta study all weekend. Big test Monday. Soooooo tired."

"All right."

We'll see.

We'll see . . .

FRIDAY MORNING RICHARD WOKE me up before leaving for work.

"Mikal, I picked up all the literature about starting classes in spring. It's on the coffee table if you wanna look it over."

"I still gotta take the GED."

"I'll help you. You'll ace it no problem."

"Man, you up for it really? Putting up with all those liberal PC assholes every day?"

"Dude, I love PC. Political correctness is one of the greatest things to ever happen to the Movement. Whenever society as a whole decides to give words more weight than they warrant? Advantage: us. Whenever people think language is our master and we're its servant and not the other way around? Advantage: us. Hell yeah I'm excited to face those douchebags every day. They've handed me all the weapons I need. Thank god for PC."

"Huh. Yeah. Plus it gives the . . . what would you call it . . . the 'respectable right' the chance to play the First Amendment martyr card."

"Exactly. See, you're catching on. You going to Meat's tonight?"

"Maybe."

"Maybe? What do you mean maybe?"

"Maybe. I'm not in a party mood. I want to talk to him. But I want to talk business."

"What kind of business?"

"Bombs. Pipe bombs. Cocktails. Chemical shit."

"Well, Meat is the man as far as that goes. He'll be excited to chew the fat about that stuff. I'll see you there tonight. Get a ride with Joey. Oh, and by the way, we're *completely* out of grub."

"I know."

SO I SPENT THE rest of Friday morning looking over college literature and thinking about bombs. It's hard to know how to feel. I didn't really feel too much.

THREE O'CLOCK ROLLED AROUND. No Sherry. Five. No Sherry. Eight thirty. No sign of her. And I thought some more about bombs.

FOURTEEN

Friday evening I took the last bus into town, got off at Fourth and Jamestown, and followed the noise from there. A "block rocker" it was indeed. Even the front yard outside the house was packed with people. As I buttoned up my flannel and adjusted my knit skullcap it occurred to me that I looked more like a longshoreman than an Aryan Warrior just then, which was certainly the right way to go. Like any self-respecting Skin of the time I loathed Seattle "grunge" rock and whatever it may have stood for, so sans red braces and geared in everyday hiking boots, I felt undercover and in disguise. *Even more anonymous than normal.* Perfect.

THINKING ABOUT IT NOW, I had to have been an imbecile walking into that house party alone and without an Uzi at least. Talk about enemy land. This was a bacchanal hosted by The Devil himself, and it was everything I had trained myself to hate. The air was thick with weed and cloves and my fear of the contact buzz had to be addressed and discarded once and for all the moment I walked in the door.

The place was loaded with multi-cultists, and they danced to rap and funk and world beat and even the heavy stuff was infected with tribal drums and third-world ooga-booga. College chatter every which way about books I had never read and issues that don't come up in my house, with my clan, around my campfire. These people were for all intents and purposes my peers, and yet they might as well have been from the Fifth Dimension. The twilight zone *or* the band. Either way. I overheard a couple of people talking about counter-protesting a demonstration by the local chapter of the Ku Klux Klan at the end of the month. Seems the Klan, in a desperate move to remind everyone they still existed, had won a permit to march on the square. *Poor, sorry, cousin-fuckin' bastards.* I did feel naked and spotlighted and persona non grata for a just brief moment until I realized just how inconspicuous, incognito, and inconsequential I truly was. And as for The Devil himself, I had sworn to end his life. But I didn't even bother to case his house for a bombing, as initially planned. I was there instead about a girl and a secret and that's just the way it was and it seemed to make sense at the time. A girl who wasn't mine. A secret with its own designs. In the house of The Devil and a one-sided holy war. Like I said, it seemed to make sense at the time.

THERE WAS A FRONT yard and a backyard, two floors plus a basement, and a couple hundred bodies to wade through. That house was as good a place as any to lose myself, and that's just what I did that night. Stands to reason, as I had already lost all sense of perspective and I must have lost my mind. I had certainly lost Sherry, as if she had ever been mine to find or keep in the first place. I didn't even know if she was there.

I wove through the crowd out to the backyard to find a large bonfire and a mammoth grill cooking up barbecue. A well-worn boom box blasted out some old-style hip-hop I recognized from my Blackchurch days. I grabbed a plastic cup, made my way to the keg, and pumped out some domestic swill.

"What can I get you, my man?" this red-headed Jew-fro'd hippie minding the grill asked me, then proceeded to sing along with the radio, "Excuse me Doug E . . . Excuse me Doug E . . . Excuse me Doug E. Fresh you're on! Uh-uh, On . . . on . . . on . . ."

I wanted to say "nothing," but I hadn't eaten all day and the fixings on the grill smelled like they had been cooked up by the Almighty.

"Well," I replied, "is this meat or, uh, like, tofu meat substitute?"

"It's fucking *meat*, dude," the hippie laughed, feigning offense and flipping a rack of ribs. "*Tofu*. Pshhh. Hey Greg, did you hear this fuckin' guy?"

"Greg," a Korean in a jester's cap and Stigmata Dog T-shirt, giggled like a moron and gave the thumbs-up. I chuckled and shrugged.

"All right. Just had to make sure. Pull me some of that pork."

"Right on right on. Get you a bun. This shit is the bomb-ditty-bomb-bomb."

??? Okay . . .

"Hey, y'all know a girl named Sherry Nicolas? I'm supposed to meet her here."

"Naw, doesn't ring a bell. Look around the house. There's a lot of smokin' *boo-tay* here tonight, so even if you don't find her . . ." They then broke into a fit of giggles. I opened the bun on my plate and saw that it was saturated with a thick, pungent goo. The hippie slopped a steaming heap of tangy pork onto my bun. "Haw yeah . . . ," he said, licking his lips.

"What's this stuff on the bun?"

"Green butter, baby. Buh-ZAM! It'll make you the happiest motherfucker in the world, dude. Guaranteed."

Aw fuck . . . Awwwww FUCK . . .

I thought about throwing it out right then and there, or maybe pretending to take a bite then tossing it away when I got back inside. But my stomach twisted and growled and demanded I eat at least a bit of it. I brought it to my lips, intent on taking just a nibble, but instead I chomped into it, munching it all down in two full bites. It was, bar none, the most delicious sandwich I had ever tasted, and if it had been seasoned with strychnine I would have done the same.

"Goddamn, bottomless pit!" the hippie hollered. "You want another?"

"No, I'm good. Shalom."

"'Kay. Whatever."

I guzzled my beer, grabbed another, and headed back into the house.

"WOW. THAT'S FASCINATING, CHAD," I heard Niani Shange say. I peered into what was probably meant to be the dining room to see her hitting a joint and passing it to this pasty, preppy neckbone in a polo shirt and sandals-with-socks. Niani wore a tight black pullover shirt and an ankle-length peasant skirt. Her hair hung in kinky ringlets, ornamented with colored wooden beads. I wondered what her hair felt like.

"Essentially," she continued, "whatchoo, whatchoo, what you are saying is . . . we can't give welfare to the poor because then they'll lose their drive to work. But . . . we MUST give welfare to corporations or else THEY'LL lose their drive to work. That's just. Wow. Brilliant. It really is."

"You're twisting my words, Niani!" The neckbone protested and coughed out a cloud of white smoke, and I felt like I would really like to get in on that conversation myself, but I quickly skittered away down the hall. I couldn't trust her to not recognize me. Unlike Jack Curry, whom I ran into head-on.

"My bad," he grunted, obviously already on his way to Blitzville. He swigged hard off a bottle of Jim Beam, and handed it, more or less, in my direction. I didn't take it, step back, or even startle, because I knew he didn't know who I was. His eyes weren't even open.

"S'cool," I said tossing on a character I just yanked out of the air. "Killer party, dog." He didn't hear a word that came out of my mouth. He also wasn't aware of the knife I had pulled out of my pocket and held up to his back. I waved the blade right around his belt line. It brushed lightly against his dreadlocks. With the sharp silver tip I made circles in the air, right outside his kidneys. *One stroke and you're dead, fucker. One stroke. One stroke.* I flipped it shut as that guy Yoshimoto turned the corner, holding a glass of milk. As it was, I couldn't have gotten away with stabbing Curry anyway. I would not have even made it to the front door alive.

"What's with the milk, son?" Curry slurred.

"We're pregnant," Yoshimoto replied defeated and re-signed. I was surprised for the moment that he didn't talk like an extra from *Godzilla*. There's just no telling.

Curry proceeded to dump a quarter bottle of whiskey into Yoshimoto's milk. Yoshimoto stared at the glass stunned and speechless.

"*Kaketsuke ippai,*" Curry said and stumbled on his way.

Kaketsuke ippai. Drink up to catch up.

Yoshimoto looked up at me for a brief moment and squinted.

"Cheers!" I said, hoisting my cup of beer. He nodded and walked off.

A wave washed over the front part of my brain and trick-led down through my body. I didn't know if it was the butter getting on top of me, or the quality of the air itself, but I felt suddenly coated in a thin slather of Novocain and encum-bered by the overall gelatin-like state of the atmosphere. The motion around me clipped to slo-mo, and I realized I was walking down the hallway in time with the music, slogging through space, knee-deep in cheese casserole. I sank into an available easy chair and shut my eyes, my head bobbing to the pulse of something reggae-esque but strangely alien.

"HEY, ARE YOU ALL right?"

I opened my eyes to see a nice little punk pixie sitting on the armrest of my chair. She was skinny and slight, just the way I liked them then, with short, spiky green hair. A thin gold ring pierced her septum.

"Gimme a sip of your beer and I'll be perfect," I said. She handed me her bottle of Killian's. I took a bigger swig than what was likely polite, but for some reason I felt entitled. Just the way it is.

"So are you a friend of Jack's?" she asked.

"Aw, hell yeah. That crazy bastard and I go way back."

"What's your name?"

"Um, Don Willis."

"Oh yeah! I've heard of you! You're a twin, right?"

"Yeah. Zary is my brother."

"Is he here?"

"Naw. He's in jail."

"For some reason, to hear Jack talk, I assumed you were black."

"Who's to say I ain't?"

"Well," she shrugged, "not me I guess."

She was the first girl I had talked to since Suzi, and I couldn't really gauge how I was doing. But that question pretty well answered itself when a boho-looking Indian girl slunk by and put her arm around my new friend's shoulder.

"Hetel," Greenie said, "*mere dost se miliye* Don Willis *aur mere dost—*"

"You know," the Indian girl giggled, "I CAN speak English, silly Billy."

"Argh! She never lets me practice my Hindi!"

"Good to meet you, Hetel," I said, trying to mask my disappointment.

"You're Don Willis?" Hetel asked. "Of the Willis twins? I thought you—"

"Was black? Yeah, I get that a lot. Hey," I turned to the green-haired girl. "Your name ain't Paige by any chance, is it?"

"Yep. Why?"

"I think you're in Women's Studies with a friend of mine. Sherry Nicolas?"

"Uh . . . okay . . ."

"Punk rock chick. She's got, like, short maroon hair with blond streaks."

"Oh yeah. *Helen Keller.* She's around here somewhere."

"Cool."

I couldn't lift my head, but I saw a very pregnant belly waddle through my peripheral vision. "Anybody seen my brother Greg?" it asked. "I'm looking for Greg Cho. Anybody?"

"Outside," I said, as I felt myself begin to hover maybe a half inch above the chair. "By the bonfire."

"Thanks." And the belly waddled away.

"Come dance with me, baby," Hetel cooed to Paige. And I spun my useless third wheel.

"Good to meet y'all," I said.

"Ditto," they chirped in unison, then proceeded to get some manner of freak on.

Nicely done, Jerk-off. First chick you try to talk up and she's a goddamn dyke. And with a tongue for the darker magenta no less.

I watched the two of them dance close together until a brighter vision caught my eye. Niani. Twisting and twirling. Surrounded by a little crowd of folks just thrilled to bask in her glow.

You're a sitting target. Keep moving. I wandered out to the kitchen to once again see Jack Curry's back. He was an easier kill this time, all alone and right by the door. He held the phone's receiver nearly half a foot from his ear and hollered, "Man, it's BUMPIN', D! And all the honeys be sayin', 'Where Daddy Molotov at?' Man, I ain't lyin'! So git yo' ass on over here. A'ight. A'ight cool. See ya in a minute. Peace."

D...D...D...D? D...

He stumbled off through the screen door to the outside and I once again missed the opportunity to carve him up like a Christmas goose. My heart was no longer in it anyway. Surprise.

A disembodied hand waved a joint in my face. I pinched it between my fingers and took a deep drag, coughing and sputtering. The hand laughed and took the joint back with a "Right on, dude!" And I heard it shuffle away singing along with the music.

"Thank you, Thing," I said, my lungs burning and itchy.

I turned around and leaned against the kitchen doorway. Two frat boys stood next to me holding up the wall. They looked so much alike they could have been the same guy in split screen (and yes, the irony of a Skinhead saying that is not lost on me).

"Hey," one said to the other, "you see that hot looking black chick? The one freak-dancing with everybody? I'mma try to FUCK that pussy tonight! I heard she's a sluuuuuuuut. Straight up cum dumpster, for real though. Some cat in Astronomy told me that last quarter she let him bang her doggie-style while . . . git this . . . she ate out his girlfriend, dude! DUDE! He was calling her all 'Aunt Jemima' and grabbing her hair and slapping her ass and shit, and she was loving it! Begged for it! GOD, let me hit that!"

I felt my heart suddenly kick into overdrive and my teeth clenched hard like a vice. My hands balled into fists so tight I thought for sure that my nails would cut my palms open. *He ain't got no business talking about her like that*. He didn't deserve to breathe her air, let alone jab his worthless cock inside her. *I'll kill you, you white-ball-cap-wearing bucket of swine vomit. I'll kill you before you EVER touch her.*

"Yeah, I'd split her like a wishbone," the other replied. "But watch out, 'cause, man, y'know that psycho grit that lives here with her? Fucking *murdered* a guy. That's what I heard. Cut his throat or blew up his car or some shit."

I'll hack you apart. You will know pain, you fucks. I'll yank your goddamn guts out.

"Hey . . . ," the second one whispered to the first, "did you hear what that guy just said?" They turned to look right at me.

HOLY SHIT!

The chatter in my head was apparently leaking out. They both glared at me, ready to pounce, and I figured I'd have to make a move. I pulled down the collar of my shirt and showed them the "white power" tattoo.

"Heads up, kids," I growled. "I'm about to make a phone call and it's about to get evil around here. I'm warning you cuz you're white brethren and I'd hate to see y'all caught in the cross fire. You might wanna amscray." So they did. And quick. Good thing too because I'm pretty sure my bones had turned to licorice rope by then, and I was truly in no state to fight. So I stood alone, wondering what the fuck that was all about anyway.

FROM THE OPPOSITE HALLWAY I watched Niani pass through the kitchen and out to the back deck. I followed her as far as the screen door and watched as she sat down on the top step behind Jack Curry. She wrapped her arms around him from behind and rested her head on his shoulder. I wanted to die. I felt a bolt of rage shoot through me before I realized that I had no right to it. Not mine to have. That's just the way it was. The yard was empty by then, and the three of us watched in silence as the bonfire died away. Finally Niani said to him, "He's coming over."

"Great."

"Y'all could finally patch things up."

"Yeah, right."

"He misses you, you know. Why else would he come?"

"Arnold? He just wants to pick up some easy sorority girl and punish-fuck her for the sins of the white man."

"That's ugly, Jack."

"It's an ugly world, Lees." I had to agree.

"That's quite a *teenage* attitude," she said to both of us. Even though I didn't exist.

"I just called Philips back. He's coming by."

"Oh. Wonderful. It'll be like a Blackchurch family reunion up in here."

"Yeah. Gats out, posse up."

"But see, I KNOW nobody's tryin' to act a fool up in MY house."

"It'll be a'ight."

I STOOD THERE PLAYING out this whole ridiculous scenario in my head wherein it was me on that step with her and not him. I'd tell her that I'd protect her and I'd never let anyone hurt her. I'd keep all the evil spirits away. *I am a gargoyle. I can be your gargoyle.* I imagined my crew skulking around, bad talking her and threatening her, and I'd fight each of them one by one. *I'll keep you safe.* In my mind I hadn't yet gotten to fighting Richard when I heard that *voice:*

"You're jealous, aren't you?"

I turned my head and Sherry stood with her face inches from mine holding up an accusatory index finger.

"Is that loaded?" I asked.

"You just had to follow me," she continued. "You can't ever leave me alone. It's cuz you're jealous."

"Why are you here?"

"Because I fell in love and I can't help that. How about you?"

"Nope."

We looked out through the screen door at the two of them sitting there. If they felt our eyes they made no show of it. The party seemed miles in the background and I stood there feeling like a stalker. *At least I ain't the only one.*

"Fuck," Sherry muttered as she watched them, her eyes welling with tears. "Fuck fuck fuck." She punched the wall with her left fist and yelped in pain, but reared back to punch again. I grabbed her wrist midair. "Let go of me, Mudhoney."

"Stop it. So what, you don't want to be with Richard no more?"

"I don't know. I don't know what I want. Well, I know what I want . . . but I don't know what to do."

"You talked to him?"

"No."

"Cuz you don't just *break up* with Richard Lovecraft, you know. I hope you understand that."

"I know."

"Especially . . . well, it don't make no difference. You just don't break up with him."

"I'm not anybody's property."

"See, that's where you're wrong."

"You want a beer, Mikal? I'm going to go get us some beers."

AND OFF SHE WENT. My entire body buzzed, and I felt my fingertips pricked with tiny plastic pins. I felt *watched*, and decided it was time for me to leave. Oriental Greg with the joker's hat came stumbling into the room saying:

"Anybody know a Mike Shannon? Mike Shannon." He turned to me and asked, "Dude, you know a cat named Mike Shannon?"

"Never heard of him. Why?"

"He's got a phone call."

Whatthefuck . . .

I headed for the front door just in time to see D'antre Philips walking in. One hundred and eighty degrees and off I went in the other direction.

Back to the kitchen, out the screen door, to the deck and ready to break into a sprint, and there she was sitting alone on the top step.

"Hi Mikal Fanon," Niani said. "It's wild that you came here." I hurried past her down the steps, out into the yard and the near pitch-dark. *Run! RUN!* "Hold up for just a minute," she said. And, dutifully, I froze in my tracks.

"You . . . can't see me," I said. "I'm invisible."

"Well, I thought ya knew I'm wearing my magic glasses today."

"Curses. Foiled again."

My head was strapped tight in on a Tilt-A-Whirl. I wanted to run away. Into the night. Into the nothing. I wanted to kiss her. I wanted to hit her for making me want to kiss her.

"I saw your folks not long ago," she said. "I usually see them in Blackchurch when I'm down visiting mine's. They're always really kind to me when I see them."

"Don't be fooled," I said. "It's just fake-friendly, Mid-western 'howdy neighbor' bullshit. I promise you, they think you're an animal."

A streak of hurt flashed across her eyes and I wanted to pull out my knife and slash my own wrists open right then and there for making that happen.

"Well"—she smiled—"they do a good job covering it up."

"Lee . . . Niani, I'm sorry I . . . I didn't wanna have nothing to do with hurting your friend, but . . . it's like . . ."

"He's fine. He's here in fact. You want to meet him?"

"No, I sure don't. And he ain't fine. I know it. That's the thing. He ain't never gonna be fine. It ain't just about damaging the body. You know that. If it was then there'd be a lot more racially motivated murders than there are. It's about *terror*. It's about scarring the *insides* all up. Setting up and maintaining the dividing lines. Perpetuating the fear and the hate. Keep it alive. Keep it burning on all fronts. The racialist's biggest fear is . . ."

"Obsolescence."

"If that means what I think it means, then yeah."

Why was I telling her this? *She's the enemy.* She was everything I had to hate. Everything . . . in one dark and beautiful package.

"You don't need those guys, Mikal."

"It's just a thing, you know. Whatever."

"You don't need them."

"You gotta . . . believe in *something*."

"Why?"

"Because . . ."

"Oh, you little boys and your plastic armies."

"It ain't . . . about that at all."

"You don't need those guys, Mikal."

I thought about Phil. I thought about myself in his place.

"I . . ." I saw myself smashed up, destroyed, and alone. "Yes . . . I . . . do."

"You high right now?" she asked.

"Yeah."

"Me too. Getting high makes me happy. So why are you so sad?"

I held up my hands to my face and was shocked to feel that it was damp. *What the fuck?* I examined the moisture on my fingertips as if I had no idea from whence it came.

"You don't need those guys, Mikal," she repeated. *She's manipulating you.*

"You ought to go stay with, with, with your parents," I stuttered. "You ain't safe here. She's gonna bring bad things to this house."

"She who?"

"Cross fire . . . you know . . ."

"What are you talking about?"

She stood up and walked slowly toward me. My chest locked shut.

"They're gonna hurt you," I whispered.

"You won't let them hurt me, will you?"

Acid tears burned rivulets down my cheeks. She slid the cap off my head like revealing a secret. I could breathe only in syncopated jags, and I was so goddamned furious at her right then. I'd spent a long time building up a good solid wall, and she burned through it like tissue paper.

"You like this music, Mikal?" I hadn't even heard it until she pointed it out.

"Yeah. It's Burning Spear, ain't it?"

"They and them does hate I . . ."

"Yeah."

And Spear sang, *"They and them does fight against I / You should see them rejoice / And tell I to run to run to run / I will never run away . . ."*

And I knew that it was just the drugs that had me shaking like a lost, cold pup . . . and she used that against me. She cradled my face in her hands and stared right into my cloudy, scarlet, salt-singed eyes.

"I . . . I . . ."

"I see you," she said.

". . . Weeping and wailing / gnashing of teeth / you got yourself to blame . . ."

"Don't touch me, you fucking NIGGER!" I grabbed her shoulders and pushed her as hard as I could. She tumbled backward, landing in the grass. "Fucking slut." I growled. "Don't trick me, you fucking dyke nigger SLUT!"

"Which is it, Mikal? Am I a dyke or a slut? You gotta pick one."

"Oh, whatever it takes. Whatever makes that money. Niggers are the fucking termites of society. Cockroaches! Feeding on filth and spreading disease. Take, take, take, breeding like sewer rats—"

"Do you even know what you're talking about? Do you understand the words you're saying?"

"Spitting out litter after litter of little niglet pickaninnies to gobble up all the fucking welfare. All the tax money! LEECHES!"

I came completely unglued. My vision was a blur. I paced around, venom dripping from my lips as tears poured out of my eyes.

"Why is it so hard for you to say that, Mikal? Why does it hurt you so bad to say it?" And she didn't break in the slightest. "Seems like you've got a job to do then. Come on. Kick me. Right here. As hard as you can."

I couldn't have stomped her even if I wanted to.

"The Jews and the socialists use the niggers as cheap labor and grunt soldiers on the front line to undermine White Christian America—"

"Here's your chance to be a hero for your race, Mikal. Stop me before I have a chance to breed like a sewer rat."

"To exhaust resources and dilute the purity of the white race through perversion miscegenation mongrelization—"

"Come on! Kick me! Kick me as hard as you can!!!"

I couldn't touch her . . .

You're hurting her! YOU'RE HURTING HER!!!

"Every new generation of a completely dependent criminal class further advances the elite Zionist agenda—" *You're hurting her! Kill yourself, you maggot!!!*

I truly did not follow my own logic at that point. The words coming from my mouth were not mine. I was a prerecorded broadcast.

"Kick me, goddamn it!"

Pull out the knife and jab it into your throat! You don't deserve to live! KILL YOURSELF!

"To usurp power from the rightful stewards of the homeland!"

"Stop me before any pickaninnies of mine can wreck your precious White America!"

I couldn't even hear myself anymore. It was all just jabbering, babbling static vibrating from my lips and buzzing in my ears. *WHITE NOISE*. Chattering, blathering meaningless words and concepts like vomiting bile, I paced and shuddered, crying and shaking like a five-foot-ten newborn. I must have stopped at some point, because after a while all I could hear were my own sobbing breaths. (And maybe a bit of Funkadelic way off in the distance.) I was broken.

"Well," she said finally, standing and brushing herself off, "I'm really glad we had a chance to have this little chat." She turned around and headed back into the house. She turned back one last time to say, "If you ever need me, Mikal Fanon, you know where to find me." And she was gone. And she won. I stumbled off through the yard to the back road. *She's still got your hat*, I thought. *Gotta get that hat back.*

I STAGGERED DOWN THE gravel alley behind the house toward Fourth Street. I felt like I had been walking for an hour at least, but it couldn't have been but a minute. I could still see the house when I turned around. I heard a voice say, "Yeah, that's one uh them that fucked Trey all up."

Out of the darkness, lurching, came two young black gentlemen of moderate build and one gigantic Magilla-looking sumbitch. The first two I recognized from the hood; the third I must have met one fateful drunken evening on the West Side. I gave an exaggerated wave.

"Hey! I guess y'all are wearing your special glasses too, huh?"

"Psssh. Damn, Shabazz, this boy trippin'."

"What up, Arnold?" I slurred. "What up, Don? Hey Don, I just softed two hoes up for you, man. No charge."

"I don't know you, punk."

"Yeah . . . that's just the way it is."

"So," Gigantor grunted, "why you gotta go messin' up my cousin Trey, huh? Lil cracka-ass cracka."

"Misunderstanding, my man. We was thinkin' he's Jewish."

I barely remember the tornado of fists. I really only felt the first blow, which opened up my cheek wound like the South Fork Dam, and turned the collar of my flannel into Johnstown, Pennsylvania. After that it was just a series of dull thuds landing somewhere near me. It was painful, but only in the abstract. I was well anesthetized. *Thank god for that Yid hippie and his drug butter. God bless that pork-dosing heeb.*

ONCE THEY GOT BORED with pounding on my lifeless shell, they headed off to the party and likely had a swell time. I spent the rest of the morning stumbling home, bloody and dazed. By the time I got to my front porch, the sun was just starting to rise, and I thought, *She's still got my hat. She's still got my hat . . .*

FIFTEEN

Walking in, I wasn't sure if I had the skill or balance just then to negotiate the obstacle course of bodies. And exactly as I had to just now to reach my den to write this, I had to creep carefully and silently over and around sleeping friends and random ne'er-do-wells (I suppose some things never change).

I was just about to my room when I heard Richard's voice.

"We missed you at Meat's last night."

"Yeah," I said turning slowly so as not to wrench my already-damaged neck. "Shit came up."

"What happened?"

"You remember them niggers that jumped us? Well, see, I went to go settle up."

"By yourself?"

"Made sense at the time."

"Did you bring a gun?"

"Meant to. But I forgot it."

"Yeah, I know. You left it cocked in my drawer."

Fuck.

"Well . . . live and learn."

"Get some sleep, Mikal. We've got a lot to discuss tomorrow. Or rather today."

"Rich, I gotta tell you something about Sherry."

"Yeah? What about her?"

Just then Sherry popped her head out of the bedroom right under Richard's arm.

"Jesus, Mikal!" she gasped. "What happened?"

Speedy little bunny ain'tya . . .

"You should see the other guy."

"What about her?" Richard asked again.

"Well . . . she wanted me to tell you that she ain't coming to Meat's party because she's got a big test Monday, but apparently you already knew that, so message delivered and I'm going to bed."

Richard chuckled, rolled his eyes, and disappeared back into the bedroom. I looked down at the floor and watched the wood panels ripple like water. I could really only see out of my left eye, and even that was hazy. My right ear rang so loudly, it would likely have been audible to someone standing nearby. Sherry emerged from Richard's bedroom holding a bottle of rubbing alcohol.

"You. Me. Kitchen. Now."

I followed as well as my busted equilibrium would allow.

She dabbed a cotton ball filled with searing hot lava against the cuts on my face. I didn't flinch.

"You look like shit, Mikal."

"Fuck you."

"Aw, whatsamatter? No joy in Mudville? Hold that ice on. It'll keep the swelling down."

"Some hot party, eh Sher?"

"Is that a threat?"

"Did it sound like a threat?"

She opened the freezer and removed a piece of steak. I watched her try not to gag as she pulled open the plastic wrap.

"I don't know if this even works or if it's an old wives' tale, but that eye is nasty, so here we go." She held the frozen steak to my eye, swallowing hard to keep the puke at bay.

"Is the steak supposed to be frozen?"

"How should I know?"

"I can hold it."

"You mind the ice pack."

"Ow!"

"Sorry." Pause. "Mikal, I said some things last night that I didn't mean to say."

"Did you *do* anything you didn't mean to do?"

"No. Did you?"

"Hell yes. Well . . . There was shit I meant to do that I neglected to. I meant to case the house. Didn't. Meant to bring a gun. Whoops. Meant to gut Jack Curry like a wild boar. Maybe next time." She drew a hard shudder-breath on that last bit, and shut her eyes tight. "So you done fell in love with that nigger, huh?"

"What?!"

"I mean that figuratively, of course. It ain't even a race thing to me no more. Nigger is a state of mind."

"Well, you should know. Good night, Mikal. Bob's your uncle."

And she padded off to bed.

"Yeah, I guess he is."

SIXTEEN

S ome party . . .
     "Wait a second. I just want to talk, Jack. Please. Can we talk?"

"Sherry . . . relax, all right? I'm not going to fuckin' hurt you."

"Don't scream at me either."

"Okay."

"And don't send me away."

"You got a lot of nerve coming around here, girl. I can see that goddamn scar on your tit from here. Sickening. Shameful."

"I'm not ashamed."

"You should be. Lot of nerve coming around here."

"Jack, I can't help who I fall in love with. I'm sorry."

"You're just . . . confused."

"I'm in love. Madly. Blindly. It's the only thing I'm sure of, and it's fatal."

"That's fucking crazy! You're with whatsisname. Dickie-boy."

"Can't I be in love with two people?"

"No. Well . . . I don't know. Can you? I can't. But we're different."

"No, that's the thing. We're not different. I know you feel exactly the same way I do. Exactly."

"I'm not in love with . . . anybody."

"Yes, you are! I know you are! And I'm sorry. I'm so sorry. I don't want to see you hurt! But you can't help the way you feel any more than I can."

"You're really fuckin' bold, you know it?"

"I feel like I don't even know who I am anymore. Do you know who you are, Jack?"

"Yeah, sure."

"Maybe I've never known. But I know how I feel right now. I've never felt so sure of anything in my life."

"Too crazy . . ."

"It ripped me apart seeing you with her tonight. It tore me up into little tiny pieces. She had her arms around you so tight and I told myself, 'It's nothing. They're just like . . . brother and sister. Right? Just old friends. Right?' But I felt like I was dying inside. I can't help that I was jealous. I can't pretend I don't feel the way I do."

"How do I know you're not going to flake like you did on that guy? I'm gonna see my whole world torn to shreds and you're just going to just . . . float on to whatever's next. Huh? Or maybe it's a set—"

"It's not a setup! I've never felt in my life the way I feel now. It's real. Don't you understand that? I don't want to *destroy your world*. I don't want anyone to get hurt. Believe me, I don't. I'm sorry."

"It's the DMC, isn't it? Quite the aphrodisiac. Power. Strength. Charisma. Devastating mind control. Gives you a panty-tickle, doesn't it?"

"You're a nasty, mean, rotten bastard. You know it? Are you proud of it?"

"No."

"Who hurt you, Jack Curry? Somebody cut you up bad."

"Wrong. Nobody touches me."

"I believe that."

"You're not the first, you know. Not even close. LOTS of girls have come before you. I've lost count."

"I realize that."

"Boys too. There have been boys. Does that bother you?"

"It doesn't make me happy. But oh well. The past has passed."

"Just so you understand."

"I'm out in limbo here. It's cold. Help me. Let me in."

"I couldn't stop you if I tried."

SEVENTEEN

I woke up to find all the guys packed tight in the front room. Every Skin in the area with whom we had even the slightest connection was there. And of course, it was a "no girls allowed" affair.

The vertigo was actually worse than it had been before I went to sleep, and the floor kept moving and dodging under me as I tried to walk. Someone handed me a beer and I handed it right back. Thankfully, at least I had regained full use of both eyes, such as they were. I found that if I didn't move them or my head at all I was fine, so after slapping a West Side newbie out of my favorite seat, I took to sitting perfectly still and trying to keep my eyes open. That's not to say that I was paying attention, however, for memories of the evening prior and the screeching and whining in my right ear dominated my focus.

Phil looked at my bruised-up, beaten-to-hell face with a knowing smile. As well as he could smile with all the wires and clamps.

"Relcome choo my 'orld, shun," he said. He gave a plaster-casted thumbs-up and resumed drinking his Foster's through a bendy straw.

"I'm glad you're all here," Richard said. "There's been

some issues bugging me lately and I thought it best that we all convene so they could be brought out and kicked about. As many of you know, the local chapter of the Ku Klux Klan, who at last count are eight strong—" An overall snicker of derision filled the room, and Richard chuckled along in agreement. "Yeah, I know, I know. Anyway, the Klan will be marching on the square next Saturday afternoon. And it's no stretch to say that this will be a great joke to a lot of the locals, and fair play to them I say. But what we sometimes forget is most people don't make the distinctions that *we* might about the Movement. So when they're laughing at the Klan, they're laughing at *us*. They're laughing at White Power. And that can't stand. I feel like we've been treading water for a long while, guys, sticking with our own and really not rising above basically thug-like behavior when we do act at all. A notable exception was Mule of The Hangmen bringing down that Baptist Church. So, respect to Mule. We will miss his great music." Richard tap-danced right on past the fact that, respect or no, Mule will not be breathing the sweet air of free- dom until he's forty-five years old. And that's providing that he actually survives Lucasville Prison. Richard continued, "I think it's time we made some tactical strikes. Hits that send a clear message that we are not playing around, and we will not be ignored. It doesn't have to happen today, this week, or even this month. But when we hit, we will hit with full power. If anyone has any good targets in mind for a strike, or even a test strike, please let us know." I could have spoken I suppose, but I kept silent.

Meat Cake's younger brother, this jittery little rat-faced boy named Stevie, got up to talk about building homemade bombs. I pretty much fazed out at that point. His wiener-dog- like yip was no match for the pounding and screeching inside my head. He started off yakking about using soda bottles as hand grenades as well as ground bombs, and he pulled up his pants legs to show the scars on his calves, illustrating what can go wrong when dealing with volatile chemicals. By the time he got to the mechanics of dousing someone with gasoline and setting them on fire, I had to excuse myself and go back to bed. I thought Richard would protest, but he just nodded, and off I went.

"I call that giving someone *the shower*," I heard Stevie say as I left. "Careful you don't get cleaned yourself."

I WOKE UP SOME hours later to find the house empty. I was able to keep the head spinning down to a workable level by walking with my neck locked into one position. I headed out back, through the rip in the fence to the grocery store. Not on my A game just then I actually *purchased* some items for a change, and came back to the house with macaroni and cheese and a two-liter of red cream soda in tow.

THAT NIGHT, AS PHIL sat in the front room watching some porno video called *Anal Virgins in BangCock*, I shaved my head with a cheap pair of clippers I had stolen the month before. *If you're gonna steal, why grab the cheap ones?* Only god knows.

"OOOOO! I COME NOW rong time rong time!" said a ridiculously over-the-top "Asian" voice.

"Sounds pretty sexy in there, Phil," I said. "It's a damn shame about your hands."

"Eat a hot dick," was his reply, and I stopped to marvel at how clear it sounded. "Eat a hot dick" may very well be the most perfect sentence to say for a person with his jaw wired shut. There's just no telling.

I didn't know it then, but that would be the last time I ever shaved my head.

———

WEDNESDAY AFTERNOON I CALLED my mom at work to see if she'd like to get together around six o'clock for coffee and a bite to eat. I hadn't seen her in a very long while and thought it might be good to catch up a bit. She said yes and we agreed to meet at a diner nearby. I got there at 5:40 and waited for two and a half hours. She never showed up.

WALKING HOME I THOUGHT about Niani. I didn't want to and I tried not to, but apparently it wasn't up to me. I couldn't shake her. *Maybe she set you up to get jumped.* But that just didn't seem true. "I see you," she said. She broke me. She called my bluff. *She called you out for the rodent that you are.* I wanted to find a way to redeem myself. Pay the fine, do the penance, *make peace.* Only with her. The rest of the world could burn away and die. But I wanted her to see me again. *Better than I am. Better than I deserve.* And I knew I had blown that chance forever.

AS SOON AS I walked in the door I could feel that something was off. Sherry's usual pile of odds and ends sat in the corner as I had come to expect, but she was nowhere in sight, and the place had an exotic aroma about it . . . both completely new to me, and yet strangely familiar. I noticed it first at the party on Jamestown Street. *Marijuana, yeah, but something else too.* A flowery soap smell that gave the air a peculiar thickness. I could hear the sounds of the Bad Brains coming from Richard's room. I knocked.

"*I love I Jah, yeah yeah / I got to keep my PMA . . .*"

"Sherry?" I tried to turn the knob, but the door was locked.

"Yeaaaah?" she drawled.

"Unlock the door."

"Come back later."

"Open up."

"I'm masturbating," she said casually. "Leave me alone."

"Come on. Open the door."

"Go away."

I commenced to knocking on the door in triplets, over and over and over, in the most irritating fashion possible. "All right, all right," she sighed. I heard her get up and pad arrhythmically across the room. The door unlatched, and I heard her pad back again. "Come on in. It's open."

"Wait a minute," I said. "Are you decent?"

"Am I *decent*? Are you queer? Come in for fucksake."

So I walked into Richard's bedroom and into a fog of white smoke. Sherry sat on Richard's bed with her eyes half-closed. She was wrapped up in Richard's Nazi flag, and all of her clothing lay on the floor in front of her.

"What's going on here?" I demanded.

"What do you mean?" she asked dreamily, her voice floaty and singsong.

"Holy fuck. I can't believe you're smoking drugs in Richard's house. He's gonna know. He's gonna murder us both."

"Richard Smichard. Bo-bitchard."

"Hmm . . . yeah . . . well, I guess I can't argue with that logic."

"Damn straight," she said. "Or not." She lifted a glass pipe to her lips and took a deep drag. She offered it to me. I declined. She shrugged and hit it again, sparking it with a lighter.

"What is that anyways? It ain't just pot."

"Shiny black rock," she replied. "It's glooooorious. Makes me tingly."

"Black rock? What the fuck is that?"

"Ooooooh peeeeeee yuuuuuuummmmm . . ."

"Oh god . . ."

"Have you ever heard of astral telepathy?"

"Oh . . . fucking *god*!"

"Me neither."

"So what, are you a junkie now? Who gave it to you? No. Wait. Don't tell me."

"Jackie gave it to me. He's a candy man."

"Yeah . . . real sweet. That's the guy who pretty much crippled your friend, remember?"

"He gave it to me to give to Phil. Said it would make him feel better. But I knew Phil wouldn't use it, so fugg'm."

"I'mma kill that guy," I said through my teeth.

"So you've threatened. Jack's pretty scaaaaary, huh?"

"Yeah . . . So, uh, are you naked?"

"I've got the flag on," she said, her eyes all a-roll. "Prude."

"Richard's gonna kill us. Why?"

"Why?"

"WHY?!"

"I *told* you, goofball. I was touching myself. Taking matters into my own hands. What, don't True Aryan Warriors ever tug on their little thingies?"

The record ended and the arm lifted up and returned to its resting place. The disc continued to spin and crackle on the wheel.

"Why don't you get dressed, Sherry? I'll make us some coffee and we'll talk some more out in the front room."

She stretched her bare legs out in front of her and stared at them, deep in thought.

"I have something not a lot of people have. A really early glamour shot of Norma Jean. Before she became 'Marilyn.' She was born with extra toes, did you know that? As soon as she was able, she had them surgically removed, and most of those early pictures with the offending digits were rounded up and destroyed. But I have one."

"Well I'll be damned."

"Yes you will. I just think it's interesting. Here she was, icon of her generation, pretty much the gold standard for beauty, but she'd had herself carved up and mutilated in order to be like everybody else."

"Yeah . . . that's just the way it is."

"Do you ever feel like you've cut off parts of yourself, Mikal? I do."

"I'm pretty well intact. Besides my hair."

"Good for you."

"Good for me."

"Do you want to kiss me, Mikal?"

"No."

"Do you want to kiss Richard?" I didn't even bother to dignify that with a response. "I know you hate me."

"Sherry, I don't hate you."

"Yes you do. You hate me because when you look at me you don't like the way you look in my reflection. You hate me for the same reason Jack hates me. Because you're afraid I've come to steal your light away."

"I think you're needin' to sober up."

"There's a select few people. Just a few, who give off a great, shining light. The rest of us can only bask, or burn, blistering, blinded, trying to dance in it."

"You are higher than weeping Jesus."

"You wanna dance, Mikal?"

"Christ almighty . . ."

"I'm sorry to say it out loud, cuz I know he doesn't want to hear it said, but I know Mikal is obsessed with Richard. More than just fond, more than impressed, he's captivated by him. He's *taken*. Richard is powerful. Charismatic. Handsome. And *evil*. *Sooooo* evil. And Mikal wants a piece of the dark light. No different from Jack Curry . . . whom Mikal *claims* to despise. Been afraid of him for years. Fear, love, worship—to Mikal there's very little difference. He's awfully Catholic in that regard."

"Or maybe you need fucking therapy. I'm standing right here. You ain't got to talk about me third person. And you don't know shit."

"Just tell me . . . honestly . . . if some night . . . by chance . . . he invited you into his bed, would you refuse?"

"You know what? Maybe I do hate you after all."

"Do you know who you are, Mikal?"

"Yeah, sure. Of course I do."

"I don't know who I am." She lowered her head and began to cry. "I don't know who I am. *I don't know who I am.*"

I stood there and let her cry. I wasn't really sure of what else to do. Looking back now, I still don't know. I eventually turned around and walked out. Took a bus to Reeba's brother's house. They had a spare room for me.

Sherry and I spoke once more on Saturday, and that was that.

EIGHTEEN

Saturday. Klan rally on the square. Torrential downpour all day. Good times.

THE DAY STARTED OFF with this message on the answering machine:

"Hi Mikal. It's Tanya. Sorry I missed you at the diner the other night. Totally slipped my mind. I ain't thinking too good these days. I would like to see you, though, so give me a call."

Tanya. It's Tanya. She couldn't even bring herself to say, "It's Mom."

I never called her back. I couldn't. That was the night that I fell off the edge of the earth.

AROUND 3:00 AM BRIAN drove me back home so I could change clothes. The house was empty, as Richard and Sherry had headed over to Meat's to rendezvous with the extended crew. Geared up and ready to roll, I picked up the phone to call my mom about a rain check. A fierce headache overtook me, a fog rolled in over my eyes, and I fell to the floor. I couldn't remember the phone number. I couldn't remember my own phone number. I grasped for any handle to pull myself upright, and ended up yanking the phone out of the wall and splitting the cord. The answering machine fell off the end table and shattered.

"Hey Mikey!" Brian yelled from the front porch. "Let's roll!"

I lay there, watching the room spin above me. Within a minute or so my head cleared and I regained my balance. *Just take it as it comes.*

WE MET UP WITH everyone down at the square, which was already packed to the splits with protesters, counter-demonstrators, and general rubbernecks. To this day I don't know what purpose we thought was served by our attendance. It did solidify a number of people's respective destinies, mine included, so I suppose the fates know what they're doing.

I HEARD NIANI'S VOICE through a megaphone: "Well, I am quite embarrassed that we've all shown up this afternoon to give so much free publicity to this pitiful excuse for a Klan march."

The crowd laughed. Cries of "you're welcome" were aimed at the Klanfolk across the street. There were exactly five of them, all dressed in their white sheets and hoods. Two men in their mid-fifties, a woman in maybe her early forties, a man who looked to be in his late nineties who was so locked in the clutches of senility that he smiled and waved to the crowd, and a young boy of about twelve. The boy was wide-eyed— enraptured with the entire scene. He appeared to feed off the negative energy, silently mouthing, "Nigger, nigger, nigger, nigger, nigger . . ." I found it rather chilling. I found it rather familiar.

Niani continued to speechify about how "love always

overrules" or some such drivel that I doubt she really believed, and it was met with warm and enthusiastic applause. She turned her megaphone over to an older black man who looked like a former prizefighter. He commenced to leading the crowd in a rousing, though somewhat confusing, rendition of "I've Got a Robe, You've Got a Robe (Goin' to Shout All Over God's Heav'n)," or so I've been told. It just sounded like nonsense to me.

A couple of the lads had taken to shouting "Sieg heil!" and goose-stepping, trying to make a scene, but the crowd was so large and preoccupied with singing that no one paid any attention.

"Knock it off, fellas," some cop yawned. "That's irritating."

WE MILLED ABOUT FOR an hour or so, cold, wet, miserable, hopelessly outnumbered, bored, and frustrated. A couple of preteens on scooters rode by and laughed at us. I couldn't tell if Richard was lost in thought . . . or just lost. He didn't even seem to realize when Sherry slipped away into the crowd. But I did. And, I couldn't help but notice, so did Phil. Since the beat down Phil's status had all but withered to nothing, and many of us wondered when the day would come that Richard would drive him out into the woods and leave him there like a useless old dog. But Phil had an air of ambition about him that day. He wasn't going to go quietly or without bloodshed.

"THIS SUCKS," RICHARD SAID finally. He turned to me and said, "Go collect Sherry. It's time to go."

"And you're thinkin' my name's Tobey? Cuz it ain't Tobey."

"What did you say?"

"You musta mistook me for a slave. But my name ain't Tobey."

"All right," he sighed. "Fine."

"It's Kunta Kinte."

"Whatever," he replied, glaring at me.

"I'll get 'er," Phil said, and trudged off into the sea of bodies.

"Guess he's not worthless after all," Richard said to no one in particular.

It occurred to me just then that shaming Richard in front of his soldiers wasn't my smartest decision ever, so I went off to assist Phil in his mission.

THUNDER CRASHED AND THE rain began to slam harder than ever. It sent many people on their way. The Klan quintet departed as well, prehensile tails between their legs.

As a large section of the crowd broke, I saw *them*. All together there huddled under an awning. And it all fell into place in my mind. I saw them: Jack Curry, Niani Shange, Yoshimoto, Lin Cho, Paige, the whole host of them. The whole lot. And Sherry, right in the middle. She looked comfortable with them. At ease. At *home*. I saw her tug on the Demon's dreadlocks, and he laughed. Niani whispered in Sherry's ear, pointing at Curry, and Sherry covered her face, *blushing*. I'd seen that maneuver before. Even from afar, I could read *that look* in Sherry's eyes. That look she used to have for Richard. That look of awe and instant devotion. *That look I shouldn't see*. I watched Sherry toss up the Nazi salute in an exaggerated fashion, and they all laughed. I should have felt betrayed, perhaps. Threatened even. *Sherry could lead them to us. They could case our house like I should've cased theirs*. But I didn't. *She's out of your reach*. I didn't feel anything. *She's a stupid little girl with a stupid little crush*. And I accepted defeat.

A small gust of fear blew briefly through me when I saw Senbe Shabazz and his Raging Black Fist! or whoever they are. But I was far enough away to not be present in their world. Shabazz chucked Curry on the shoulder as he walked by. Curry chucked him back. It was casual. Friendly even, but noncommittal. The black army marched away. I felt as though I were watching it all on television. I may as well have been.

"SHERRY!" we all heard Phil bellow. "SHERRY NICO-LASH!" He was far enough away that he couldn't be seen yet, but the third "SHERRY!!!" was closer. And the fourth closer still. She quickly gave them all hugs, lingering on Niani long enough for Niani to whisper again in her ear. Sherry nodded, and then she darted off. Away she ran, and I circled around the perimeter of the square to try to head her off.

"I WAS LOOKING FOR you!" I shouted as I ran up to her.

"Surprise," she replied.

"Let's just—"

"Bark like a good little puppy, Mikal. Bark for your master. Fetch, boy! Fetch!"

And from out of the ether Phil appeared.

"It'sh time to go. Rishard wantsh to shee you, Sherry. Get going."

"Ooooo," she said waving her arms in mock hysteria. "Best not keep *His Highness* waiting." And off she went. I began to follow her when Phil stopped me.

"It'sh over, Mikal," he hissed under his breath. "I'm blowing the whishle."

"Huh?"

"I know you've been following 'er. I know you've been watching 'er. Cuzh I've been watching you."

What the fuck . . .

"You'd better start making some sense, Phil. Clock's ticking and I'm tired of getting wet."

"I've been watching. I know pretty mush everything you know. And I think it'sh time for shome people to die. Don't you think death ish calling, Mikal?"

"Phil, what are you—"

"Why didn't you tell Rishard?!" he demanded, shaking. "About her? About *HIM*?! That cockshucker who did thish to me!" he indicated his face. "Why have you been keeping shecretsh?"

"I . . . I . . ."

"Who are you protecting?" He grasped his mouth with his fingertips, wincing in pain. Apparently trying to holler with a broken jaw is none too pleasant.

"I . . ."

"Doeshn't matter. *I'm* telling 'im. Tonight. I'm telling 'im everything I know. And I don't think Rishard's going to be too pleashed with you."

Maybe I should have been worried, but instead I was merely irritated. *Go die, Short Bus.* And being smacked by stinging rain and damp wind helped not a bit.

"Fuck it. I don't care. Earn your little brownie points if you want to, you pathetic gimp. So yeah, I know who crippled you. I hope he gets what's coming to him. Meant to bring it up before, slipped my mind. Whoops. Oh, and Sherry's got wandering eyes behind Richard's back? Fuck her. I hope she gets hers too. I don't care about her, I don't care about that rope-headed tat freak or his nigger cohorts, and I don't care about *you*."

"But," he growled, "there ish shomebody you DO care about." From out of his jacket pocket he pulled the party flyer. *Jamestown Street. Come one, come all!* My heart stopped cold.

"You . . . leave her out of this, Phil."

"Why the conshern?"

"Fuck you. She don't matter none."

"Nigger dyke with a big mouth. Sheems like a good hit to me."

"No. Leave her be."

"Two birds, one shtone."

"Look, Curry's who you want. We'll catch him on the street somewhere. Do him proper. I know where his family lives at. We'll case his mama's place, okay?"

"Too complicated. Too long to wait. I want to hit 'im now."

"Stay away from that house, Phil. I'm telling you. You stay the holy fuck away from her."

"Whatsha matter, Mikey? Little monkey twat caught your eye? Don't you like the way black shkin burnsh?"

I dove at him head-on and tackled him to the concrete. He screeched like an animal as I forced both of my hands down against his mouth. His blood oozed out between my fingers and washed thin in the rain, dissipating into the cracks in the sidewalk.

"I'LL KILL YOU, PHIL! I'LL KILL YOU BEFORE YOU HURT HER!!!"

He smashed the plaster cast on his left wrist full on into my temple, and the fragile little stones in my ear that balance my equilibrium dislodged once again. The universe tumbled and crashed about me as I pummeled his face and stomach with my fists. Somebody lifted me up at my abdomen. I saw Geoff and Brian help Phil to stand and with all my strength I kicked out and slammed the heel of my left boot square into Phil's jaw. It impacted with a sickening CRUNCH as his metal wires popped. He screamed with a spray of crimson that splashed across Brian's face. Phil spun one-eighty on the rain-slick sidewalk. Brian froze in horror as Phil's blood ran down his cheeks and forehead. We all watched Phil loping away down the street, groaning and wailing all the way. Joe started to chase after him but Richard stopped him short.

"Let him go, Joey. He's finished. There's nothing left for him anyway."

I never saw Phil again.

(IF YOU'RE READING THIS, Phil, I hope you realize that I may have saved your life that day.)

I EXPECTED IMMEDIATE STATIC, but it never came. No one said a word to me. *Stomping a cripple. It don't get much more Skin than that.* As we walked back to the cars, a cop approached Richard and said, "You'd outta keep better control over your children, Richie."

"Yes, Mr. Hansen," Richard replied, and the cop strolled away. Richard patted me on the back and said, "See ya later." I nodded and got into Brian's car with Reeba, Geoff, and Jennie. I watched Richard and Sherry kiss in the pouring rain before they got into Meat's LTD.

Brian was too freaked out to drive, so Geoff drove us back to Reeba's brother's house. "Goddamn, goddamn, goddamn," Brian muttered the whole way home, furiously wiping at his face trying to rub all of Phil's blood away. He did not succeed. "Goddamn. Goddamn, goddamn."

NINETEEN

The storm raged on the rest of the night. I drank a couple of beers, which did nothing to ease my vertigo, and went to sleep in Reeba's niece's room. I lay there with my eyes closed for an hour, maybe more, trying to ignore the spinning room. Trying not to think about Niani. About her smile. Her voice. That sad, hurt look in her eyes. I wanted to tell her that I was sorry for what I said to her. That it was all bullshit. *Just one more chance. Please.* I just wanted to be close to her one time, like Jack Curry on the back porch steps. Like Sherry at the square. *Just once. Let me just hold you one time.* I wanted to tell her that I'd begun my campaign to protect her from the evil spirits. *One down, however many to go.* But I never would. I thought about going to the house. I had missed the last bus, *but I could walk. I could walk to Jamestown . . .*

I HAD MISSED THE *last bus, so I walked to Jamestown,* Sherry said.

Sherry and Richard had been dropped off at the house. She begged him to take her back to her dorm.

"Car is at Meat's, babe," he said. "We'll get it in the morning."

Richard then proceeded to get drunk and pass out on the

couch listening to Wagner. She was stranded. Last resort of last resorts, she thought to call her roommate Sarah, but the phone was destroyed, yanked from the wall.

SO AROUND ABOUT ELEVEN o'clock, Sherry wrapped herself in Richard's jacket and headed out into the storm.

Lightning had knocked out most of the streetlights. No stars, no moon, just the cold black of the night and the hard, brutal rain. But she walked. All the way to Jamestown.

Within a mile, her boots were full and heavy, gushing over with freezing water. She tried to resist the urge to yank them off, but gave in before long.

SHERRY SAID:

I sat down on the curb, pulled off those worthless clompers with their stupid swastikas painted on, and dumped them and my socks into a trash can. My bare feet froze numb, I couldn't feel my toes, I could barely feel the sidewalk.

It was worth it.

That was the first night that we ever made love.

MEANWHILE, I TRIED TO get some sort of rest at Reeba's brother's place. To no avail.

"Mikal, wake up."

Reeba nudged me awake, whispering, her voice warbling with panic. "Come on, Mikal. Please."

"What? What's the deal?"

"Shhhh! Whisper. Richard's here. Something's *wrong*. I don't know what's going on, but it's bad. Oh god, it's bad."

I looked her over. She was wearing a large men's-size, button-down shirt, and nothing else. Her lip trembled, her eyes floated in deep pools of fear.

"Where's Brian?"

"He's sleeping. Geoff and Jennie went home. I was just sitting there watching TV when Richard came banging on the window. Whatever he's plotting, I don't want Brian involved."

My stomach knotted.

"What hc's plotting?"

"He's crazy, Mikal. He's not acting himself. He barged into the house, demanded I wake you and Brian up, and then smashed an ashtray with his fist. Then he called Meat, left this horrible message about burning people to death, and now he's sitting out there in a rage waiting for Meat to call him back. He's just sitting there shaking, muttering to himself over and over. You've got to stop him! I don't want Brian mixed up in this. Whatever it is. You've got to do a better job than I did." She put her face in her hands and began to cry. She pulled the shirt down to cover her nakedness. "He didn't want what I offered. He just pulled my hair real hard and called me a 'gutterslut.' I'd do anything to protect Brian! Anything. I don't want to lose him."

"What's he muttering?"

"It's awful."

"What's he saying?"

"'Kill the bitch. Burn her. Kill that fucking cunt bitch.' Something. Does he mean Sherry? Why? Why is he going to kill Sherry?"

"He's not talking about Sherry."

TWENTY

Shuddering, wobbling and numb below the ankles, drenched, and chilled to the bone, Sherry finally made it to the house on Jamestown Street. Before she could so much as ring the bell, the door flew open.

"Hurry quick inside!" Niani said. "Before you get pneumonia." She didn't have to tell Sherry twice. "You didn't walk here, did you?" Niani asked. Sherry simply shivered in reply. "Well, why didn't you call?"

"Ffff . . . ffff . . . phone's b-b-broken," Sherry stuttered, her teeth chattering. "No car."

"Damn, girl . . ."

"But it's . . . it's all g-g-good!"

"Oh . . . kay . . ."

Jack was away at work. The late shift. Sherry knew that. That's why she came. That's why she walked. Through a hard, metallic rainstorm. Like needles shot out of a cannon.

"N-nice p-p-p-place you got."

"I'm glad you're here, but, you didn't really need to . . ."

I would have swum through magma to be with you, Sherry thought. *I would have crawled on broken legs.*

"Come on upstairs. Let me find you a towel or a blanket."

———

I LOVE YOU. I love you.

NIANI WORE GRAY SWEATPANTS and a Malcolm X T-shirt, wooden bracelets, and silver rings. Somewhere in the house Nina Simone sang on a vinyl record.

"Black is the color of my true love's hair . . ."
I wanted to kiss her so badly, but I didn't know how to go about it.

"GIRL," NIANI SAID, "WE need to get you out of those clothes."

Sherry gasped. "Wh . . . what?"

"They're soaked. Go take you a super-duper hot shower. I'll put that stuff in the dryer and make us some cinnamon tea, all right? Sound good to you?"

Good to me . . .

SHERRY CRANKED THE SHOWER dial as far to the left as she could stand.

I felt the chill drain out of my bones, from the top of my head all the way down my body and out the tips of my toes. I'm in love with you, *I thought.* How do I tell you that I love you? *I didn't want to frighten her. I didn't want her to think I was crazy.* But I was! You make me crazy. *From the moment I laid eyes on her I loved her. I couldn't help it.* I'm out of my mind. *It was out of my hands. I fought it. I lied to myself about it. Tried to convince myself that I couldn't, she wouldn't, it's impossible, over and over and over and over.*

THROUGH THE GLASS SHOWER door Sherry saw Niani's silhouette enter the bathroom and place a stack of fresh towels and some manner of dry things for her to wear. She stood perfectly still for a moment, soapy and poised, knowing Niani was watching her. *I hope you like what you see.* Apparently she did. But like a lady, Niani quickly turned on her heel and left.

And Sherry forgot, for a while, all about Richard.

Which was a dreadful mistake.

TWENTY-ONE

I walked out to the living room to find Richard pacing about.

"Beautiful night, eh Rich?"

"Go wake Brian up."

"Reeba says no."

"Reeba can suck my dick."

"Wasn't that on the table already?"

"Shut the fuck up and go get him. I'm not playing around." The phone rang and he snatched it right up before it completed the first chime. "Meat? Yeah, you heard me right. Bring it all. Whatever you got. Call everybody. Everyone needs a piece too. This is no joke. I'll see you in forty." And he hung up.

"I ain't carrying no gun, Richard. You know that."

"Mikal . . . You're a very small man. I suggest you don't stand in my way."

"Tell me what's going on."

"WHY DON'T YOU TELL ME!!!"

"What?"

"You're the guy who knows everything, right?!"

"I don't know nothing."

Brian came stumbling out of the bedroom half-asleep, Reeba trailing behind him.

"What's goin' on out here?" He yawned, squinting.

"Nothing, baby," Reeba said. "Mikey and Rich are just leaving. Come back to bed."

"Get dressed, Brian," Richard said. "We've got business."

Without a blink or a question, Brian hurried back to the bedroom.

"Please, Richard," Reeba begged. "Please let Brian sit this one out."

"Mikal, would you shove something in this cow's maw so I don't have to listen to her?"

"I hate you," she cried. "I *hate* you."

"I don't even know what the deal is," I said.

He removed the tattered remains of the flyer from his pocket. It was so faded and rain damaged that it was hardly legible. "You know this house, Mike?"

"No."

"How could you lie to me like that?"

"I . . . I mean, I've been there. But—"

"Well, you're going there again. And we're having a bar-becue." He pulled out a small handgun and presented it to me. *No.* I didn't budge. "You really don't want to defy me right now." Nothing. *I can't.* "Don't go breaking my heart." *God . . . no . . .* "I'm not telling you again, Mikal." I took it and shoved it into my pocket. Brian returned fully dressed, and Reeba grabbed his arm.

"Brian," she sobbed. "You don't have to go. This isn't going to—"

"Brian," Richard interjected, "I think it's time you dumped that used cum sack out on the curb with the rest of the gar-bage. Those holes were worn out busted and spent back when *I* had her."

Reeba's face scorched up bright scarlet and tears streamed down her face. "You bastard," she spat. "You fucking bastard."

"Drop the wench, Brian," Richard continued. "You don't need it. There are better whores out there with way less cock damage."

Brian looked at Reeba.

"Brian, no . . . ," she cried.

"Look at her. Look at her stomach. She's swallowed so many loads she's getting spunk fat. Lose her."

"Okay, Richard," Brian said. "I will. Bye, Reeba."

And with that we left. I heard Reeba collapse to the floor, sobbing, as we walked out the door. I never saw her again.

TWENTY-TWO

Wiping a bit of condensation from the mirror, Sherry inspected her tattoo. It was rough and hideous. Artless and spotty. *Embarrassing.* She chuckled to herself when she saw the clothes that Niani had left for her: a pair of men's boxer shorts that must have been Jack Curry's, and a tight black T-shirt. It read: The Blacker The College The Sweeter The Knowledge.

SHERRY JOINED NIANI ON the couch in the upstairs living room, where she was greeted with a mug of piping-hot tea . . . *which I proceeded to spill on myself like a clumsy dork.* Niani giggled. Sherry's heart slammed around inside her chest. She felt dizzy. Niani got up to drop a new platter on the turntable. This time it was Ella Fitzgerald's turn, and she sang:

"*I tremble at your touch . . .*"

"So . . . um . . ."

"Yeah . . ."

"*I want you oh so much / I know I shouldn't / but that's the way it is . . .*"

"It's quite a . . . a thing, you know?"

"For real."

"Quite an evening."

"Pretty wild day overall."

"So . . ."

"Yeah."

"Yeah . . ."

Sherry thought about making a break for it. *I thought about running away. For the second time in one night. Barefoot. In freezing rain. And pitch-dark. Half-naked, in men's underpants, and with no where to go. I considered it.*

"It's really . . . cold . . . outside."

"Uh huh."

Sherry didn't know what to expect to happen. She blew on her tea and swayed to the music. Niani took a sip of her tea. Sherry did likewise and burned her mouth.

"You okay?" Niani asked.

"Yeah . . ." *I felt like an idiot.*

Niani sang along with Ella. Sherry swayed back and forth to the soft, shuffling rhythm. *I wanted to . . . talk to her. I needed to talk to her. But about what?* So instead she intently sipped at her tea as if that's all she wanted to do.

Sherry had watched Niani at school, on stage, out and about, so confident and sure in front of hundreds of strangers. She always seemed so radiant and in control and one step ahead of the rest of the world. But on that couch, she seemed so small. *Tiny . . . just like me . . .*

"Thank you for inviting me over."

"Thank you for, you know, coming."

"I'll love you forever / though it may never be / but that's the way it is / with people like you and me . . ."

"Wow," Sherry said. "That's a sad song."

"You want me to change the record?" Niani asked. "I could put something different on."

"No, it's pretty. I like it."

"You sure? I got lotsa stuff."

"Uh uh. It's good."

But then, alas, the very next tune started in with lady Ella, in no uncertain terms, begging her lover to *"Make love to me, my darling . . ."*

Oooooooooh my . . .

"Uh, so," Sherry interjected over the lyrics, "what's up with this guy?"

She indicated a large framed black-and-white photo hanging on the wall of an odd-looking black man with wild, silver hair. Bayard Rustin as it turns out. Gay. Black. Communist. Friend of MLK's. *Who knew?*

"He's a hero of ours," Niani said. "Jack's and mine. We decided we needed one good icon for the wall in here."

"Must I extend an invitation / to make love to me, my darling . . ."

"Of course," Niani continued, blushing if she could blush, "Jack campaigned for Harriet Tubman because she, quote, 'led her people to freedom with a gun to their heads,' unquote. He bought this huge painting of her at a flea market. But she seems a little, I dunno, obvious, yeah?"

"I've got hero posters on my walls too," Sherry said.

"Who do you have?"

"Just old dead people."

"Of course."

"That's an impressive record collection you've got here," Sherry said, still attempting to deflect attention away from Ella laying it all out. And indeed it was. Twice the size of Richard's, if not more.

"Ah . . . vinyl," Niani sighed. "Why listen to anything else?"

They sat speechless, again, sipping at their cinnamon tea, letting Ella do the talking. After a good while, Niani stood up and walked over to her record wall. Flipping through the discs she began to dance to the music . . .

"*Before the mood that I'm in changes—*"

"Sherry?"

"*Make love to me—*"

"Yes?"

"*Make love to me—*"

"You want to dance?"

"*My darling . . .*"

"Uh . . . no. I—"

"Yes you do."

"No I really—"

"Yeees you dooooo."

"*I'm so—*"

"I . . ."

"*In love—*"

"Dance with me."

"*With youuuu.*"

"I got two left feet."

"But they're such pretty left feet."

I'M SO IN LOVE *with you.*

"Okay."

SO THEY DANCED. SLOWLY. Each song inching closer and closer together . . .

And by the time the album was through, I was not only mad for her, I wanted to sleep with Ella Fitzgerald as well. She smelled like heaven. She tasted even better. And when she led me by the hand down the hallway to her bedroom, I had to follow. I would follow you anywhere. Holding her body against mine, smoldering-hot and delicate and smooth as wet silk, I felt the woman I had been, whomever she was, melt away into nothing. Goodbye, and good riddance to me.

Oh god did she ever make love to me that night . . . Never felt anything like it. Only the finest opium can come close . . . and even that's a bunch of jive.

I'd been searching for a shining light to dance in, to bask in, and she was the brightest I've ever seen. A golden fire that would shimmer, sparkle, shine, or ignite, shaming the rays of the sun itself. I couldn't help but be drawn in . . . even if it meant burning alive.

Niani . . . my love . . . I'll forever be dancing in the light of you.

TWENTY-THREE

Bullet rain pelted the sides of Meat's LTD. It seemed to fly at us from all sides, rocking the wagon like a tugboat lost at sea. Some neighborhoods were even without streetlamps. We were a caravan of three station wagons and four large vans. An army, setting off to wage holy war on a tiny, oblivious, unprepared enemy. Death rode on the wind like smoke and napalm.

"MIKAL," RICHARD ASKED, EXAMINING the address on the flyer, "is this a four or a nine?"

"It's a nine."

"Four it is."

"Whatever."

Meat drove. Geoff rode shotgun. And as we hit the first red light rolling into downtown, he threw open the passenger-side door and ran off into the night. No one blinked. Meat leaned over, shut the door, and away we went.

"So long, Geoff," Richard said to himself. "For your sake I hope we never meet again."

TWENTY-FOUR

Somewhere far, far away Sherry thought she heard Etta James singing "Tell Mama." *But that may be just my imagination.* Mostly she just heard her own heartbeat, and her deep, contented breaths. *And hers . . .*

"So . . ." she said finally, "your real name is Lisa Johnson?"

Niani chuckled. "There are only two people in the whole world who call me 'Lisa.' My grandmama and Jack. I wasn't born with my *real* name."

THEY LAY IN BED cuddled close together, sharing a large Santa-head mug of white Zin.

"Sorry for the mug. It's all I could find that's clean."

"Cool with me."

"It's so inelegant."

"Hey, this is classy where I come from."

"Yeah . . . me too, actually."

Niani took a sip and handed it to Sherry. She gulped it too fast and coughed. Niani giggled and smoothed Sherry's sweat-soaked hair. "You can too, if you want to. You can call me Lisa."

"No, that's okay." Sherry smiled and kissed her. "I love

Niani. So beautiful." She attempted another drink, but her fingers were slippery with perspiration, and she ended up spilling it on herself. "Aw, Christ!" Wiping her bare chest with her hand, she had to look once again at that hideous black scar that mocked her from her left breast. "Figured no point in trying to hide this from you," Sherry said softly. "But I swear, I'm going to get it lasered off as soon as humanly possible. I promise."

"No. Don't, Sherry. Don't ever get it removed. Scars are important. They remind us were we've been. You know? Don't tamper with the map."

Niani leaned her head down, gliding her lips across Sherry's skin, tracing the broken cross with her tongue. *Ohh-hhh . . . sweet Jesus . . .*

"Mmmmm," Niani cooed. "Zinfandel."

THEY HEARD THE BACK door slam and decided it was probably time to get out of bed. Niani put on her sweatpants and a robe. Sherry got back into the T-shirt and boxers, and they headed downstairs to investigate.

DOWN IN THE KITCHEN they found Dave Yoshimoto and Jack, dripping wet, rummaging through the cupboards like mangy street mutts.

"Fuckin' starvin'," Jack said.

"Aren't you supposed to be at work?" Niani asked.

"Fuck 'em."

"Fair enough. Hey Dave. You want a beer? You remember Sherry?"

"Yes, I would like a beer and yes I remember Sherry. Hey Sherry. Good to see you again."

"Ditto. When's your baby due?"

"Any day now," Dave answered.

"Are those my boxers?" Jack asked.

"You know I've been dying to get into your shorts, Jackie," Sherry said. Everyone laughed.

"Keep 'em," he said. "Don't say I never gave you nothing."

"I would never say that."

DAVE AND NIANI RETIRED to the front room with their respective beverages. Sherry was about to follow when Jack Curry put his hand on her shoulder.

"Happy?" he whispered in her ear.

"Very."

"Scared?"

"Very."

"Cool. You should be. On both counts. Just listen up. That's my girl in there. Love of my life. My Siamese twin, okay? I've got a good feeling about you, so I'm happy for you. But you ever do something to hurt her, you bring any kinda pain down on her, and we fightin'. Ai'ight?"

"Ai'ight," she answered, *but it sounded stupid coming out of me.* She turned around and hugged him tight, his long, soaking-wet hair enveloping her like a drenched curtain. "Thank you, Jack."

"Um . . . okay . . ."

And just at that moment a Molotov cocktail smashed through the front window, shattering against the living room wall and setting the sofa ablaze.

TWENTY-FIVE

Outside, rocks and bricks flew overhead toward the house as lightning flashed across the sky. The storm raged and the Fifth Reich marched into battle. Using the party flyer, Richard lit another cocktail and heaved it through a downstairs window.

"Someone station the back of the house," Richard said.

But there was little cohesion to the operation. More cocktails followed. No one drew a gun as yet, and the taunting and screaming of epithets was kept, surprisingly, to a minimum. At first. They were trying to draw the inhabitants out. I thought about Niani. I thought about Sherry. And I hoped that they had already left. *Run.* I could only stand by and watch. *Worthless.* Stevie pulled a tank of gasoline from the back of an old blue van. Richard nodded to him.

"First person you see come out gets the shower."

This was certainly a fork in the road. *The fates have laid the paths, and we flip a coin and move.* A moment of still fell across the yard, and I'd like to think everyone contemplated for that moment the commitment they were making just then. *There's no turning back from this.* Is this truly what everyone wanted? *Is this the revolution?* I'd like to think everyone gave it a second's thought, but perhaps it was only me. How many armies have marched off to kill and die on such flimsy pretense as this? How many wars have been waged over backed-up jism, blue balls, and a bruised ego? *All of them. All of them.*

"YOU KNOW," I OFFERED finally, "there is a back door . . . and a gravel road at the bottom of the hill."

AT THAT MOMENT, JACK Curry came flying out the front door, shirtless and wild, .357 aimed right at us, as a troop of armed black men emerged from behind the house. Guns at the ready. Senbe Shabazz in front. Skins all drew frantic pistols. Some ducked behind cars. Most, like Richard and I, were caught exposed in the open air. Instinctively I pulled the snubnose from my pocket and set it dead aim on Curry. Richard did the same. And as the thunder crashed right on top of us and the house fire roared against the night, we all faced off like opposing chess pieces.

"Do I know you, Hippie?" Richard asked Jack Curry. Jack laughed.

"You're staring down the barrel of a fully loaded .357 Colt Magnum Carry. Do I really look like a fucking hippie to you, Cro-Mag?"

"No sweat, lads," Richard said to us. "Like shooting monkeys in a barrel."

"Uh, excuse me, Mr. Shabazz?" Curry asked, as cocksure and snide as the Morning Star.

"Yes, Mr. Curry?" Senbe replied.

"Your men here, they're all trained marksman, yes?"

"Why yes, Mr. Curry, certified sharpshooters every one."

"Oh fuck, Rich!" someone jabbered in a panic. "Oh fuck!"

"Tsk tsk. Not looking too rosy for you, Mr. Lovecraft," said Curry. "Not too rosy." His cool veneer cracked open right then, and he yelled, "You hear me, Dickie?! You're gonna die for pussy tonight! Girl got heroin in her snatch? Was it worth dying for? All you baldy-roughneck-knuckleheads are gonna die bleeding and shitting yourselves cuz your dude here lost his pussy!" And he laughed this hideous, staccato laugh.

Die, you fuck.

"Say there, houseboy," Richard said to Shabazz, "yo' massa sure likes to surround himself with lotsa black cock, doesn't he? Does he make you suck him? Guess he wasn't getting much off that dyke mammie he had housed up here, huh? What's it mean to you? He feed your crack habit? This'll all be over if you tell me where—"

"SHE'S GONE!!!" Jack bellowed. "YOU LOST HER!!!"

AND I WONDER TODAY, if he was talking to Richard, or himself.

He could have been talking to me. *She's gone. You lost her.*

WITHOUT REALIZING WHAT I was doing, I moved my aim—up to then trained directly on Curry's face—to the back of Richard's head. Snapping to, I quickly moved my focus back to Curry. But the muzzle drifted again to Richard's skull. *You can stop him. You can't let him hurt her.* Back to Curry. *Point it at yourself.* The pouring rain made my trigger finger slippery.

SUDDENLY, THE YARD WAS awash with floodlight, sirens blaring, and rollers spinning. Cruisers and meat wagons screeched onto the scene as police jumped from their vehicles, weapons drawn. Fire engines came wailing up the backstreet behind the house just in time for the building to collapse in flame. The officers hollered for everyone to drop their weapons and hit the ground. My head slipped from its axis as the scene became a wash of noise. It became television. A vaudeville show. A staged moment strictly for my observation. *I am not party to it. I'm invisible.*

The stalemate remains. The cops scream their final warnings.
"All of you! Drop your fucking guns now!"
No one moves.
"We will be forced to open fire!"
Nothing.
The rain falls to a steady pour. The thunder subsides.
"This is your last chance!"
Last chance.
Last . . . last chance . . .
Last chance . . .
Then it starts. A gun falls to the mud. And then another. And another. Gradually, one by one, everyone drops his gun and lies flat on the ground. I do. Meat does. Joe does. Stevie does. Shabazz does. All his men do.

I forget why we are there in the first place. None of these people are familiar to me. Something about a girl. I don't know which one. I know I loved a girl once. I think I did. Don't know her name. Maybe I used to know. Maybe I just saw her picture one time and made the whole thing up.

WE ALL LAY ON the ground and put our hands out flat. Only Jack and Richard remained standing; their weapons still pointed at one another . . .

"You two, drop the fucking guns!"
"Drop 'em now!"
"Drop 'em and get down!"
"I know your parents, Richie! Don't do this!"
"This is your last fucking chance! Drop 'em or we open fire!"

———

THEY WON'T GIVE IN. Neither one of them will submit. They will never surrender.

"OKAY!" JACK HOLLERED SUDDENLY. "Okay . . . it's all over now!"

He slowly began to lower his gun to set it on the ground. *Could he really accept defeat? Could he?*

But before that pistol left his fingers I would swear on Tanya's eternal soul, whatever it's worth, that Curry flashed Richard one last murderous look and that barrel was aimed right for him. Richard pulled his trigger, and the bullet smashed through Curry's thigh, shattering his femur.

The police line lit up on Richard . . .

Lucifer . . .

And I watched my best friend fall to the ground in a spray of gunfire . . .

The harbinger of light.

Each shot a cloud of powder, a spurt of crimson, a sprinkling of pulverized bone.

CURRY DID NOT DROP his gun and instead lay on the ground, twitching, gurgling, waving his weapon in the air. A cop's bullet tore through his wrist, dropping the gun to the grass. Another officer ran up and bashed him in the head with a baton to subdue him. White as death. Gasping and gurgling in heavy shock. But he would *survive*.

SHERRY SAID:

Everything after the first firebomb is such a blur in my memory. Jack called Senbe. The living room burned. Niani and Jack screamed at each other. Smoke and fire. Jack refused to leave the house. Dave grabbed Niani and picked her up,

*dragged her through the back door kicking and screaming. I
sobbed. Followed close behind. And we ran ran ran. To Dave's
car and gone. We heard the gunshots far in the distance. Niani
screamed JACK! She cried WE GOTTA GO BACK FOR
HIM! Sat in the back seat. I cradled her in my arms crying,
Please don't leave me. Please don't leave me. Dave drove us to
his apartment. Safe harbor. I knew Richard was dead. And I
didn't know how to feel.*

RICHARD AND JACK CURRY were loaded into an ambulance as the rest of us were handcuffed and tossed into the
backs of waiting cruisers and meat wagons. I felt the metal
cuffs clamp onto my wrists behind my back, and I was lifted
into the air by unseen hands. I shut my eyes to stave off the
spinning as I was dropped into the back of a cruiser alone,
freezing and drenched, caked in mud and gravel. I heard Jack
screaming, "I'm sorry, Arnold! I'm so sorry!"

Shabazz's voice replied, "Jack! Stay up, brotha! Keep strong!"

A cop said to him, "Shut the fuck up, boy," and there was
no more Senbe to be heard.

"I'm sorry, Arnold! I'm sorry!!!" and the ambulance door
slammed shut and we all disappeared into the night.

I LAY CURLED UP in the back of the cruiser, feeling every
bump in the road. My mud-and-rain-soaked face glued to the
vinyl seat. *Ah . . . vinyl . . .*

I knew Richard was dead. And I knew Jack Curry would
live. And all I could think was that Richard was the strongest
man I'd ever known. He was the bright light. The shining star.
*That Richard's just got a way about him. Richard's just got a
way.* The brightest. The quickest. The living Power. And even
he couldn't bring The Devil down.

———

SHERRY SAID:

I grieved for a long time, Mikal. Believe that I did. I was hurt and I was guilt-ridden and I was furious. I was angry at him. And I hated him. And I missed him. And I was angry at myself for thinking that the world was better off without him. I still am. And I still do.

Mikal, I'm so sorry. Please don't hate me. I know you loved him. I know how much you loved him. And I understand. We love the wrong people sometimes. That's just the way it is.

TWENTY-SIX

We all did time. All of us. Surprise. Some did harder time than others. I don't have to tell you which people those were, do I?

"Them people just can't catch a break, can they!"

THERE WAS SOME DEBATE about whether or not I should be tried as an adult. I was not yet eighteen, but my involvement in the incident, the extent of my trespass . . . and so forth. I ended up being tried as a juvenile which, more than likely, saved my life. It's not that juvie was a day at the Magic Kingdom, but some of my old crew who went to big boys prison are dead right now and they left bad looking corpses and that's just the way it is.

AFTER THAT NIGHT, I never saw any of them again. I didn't visit anyone. I didn't keep in touch with anyone. I don't to this day. Thinking about it now, I can't even remember how each of them looked individually. In my memory they're all just slight variations on a theme. I doubt I'd recognize any of them on the street today. I don't even recognize me.

I'd heard through a tangle in the grapevine that Phil
Reider and Joe Briggan both attempted to enlist in the Army.
Phil did not pass the physical and today works as a mechanic
in Cleveland. He's married and has a daughter with cerebral
palsy. Joe successfully joined up and just recently returned
home from combat in Iraq in multiple pieces. He's alive,
more or less, and does have most of one arm left.

ALL TOLD, I WAS a Skin for barely a year. And yet, it's
the thing that I carry. It defines me more than anything else.
Sixteen. Seventeen. Most folks wear a thousand hats during
that time, trying to find out what fits them best. No consid-
eration, no contemplation, just dive in and try it out. Most
are discarded and folks move on. I happened to have worn
a costume with consequences. So I continue to carry it with
me. That's just the way it is.

I COULDN'T POINT TO a specific spot on my personal timeline where I stopped being a True Aryan Warrior. I just became,
gradually over time, less true. It was difficult in juv, because
there were baby Skins there already, and I was a legend.
    "There he is. That's Richard Lovecraft's right-hand man.
He was with him *that night*. RAHOWA!"
    I kept my distance from them as much as possible. One
particularly zealous fan ended up with a broken nose. My
officially stated reason for punching him was, "He begged me
to let him suck me off." Which was, in fact, the truth.

I SPENT MY FIRST month and a half perpetually in the
doghouse for fighting. The worst was with a trio of Chicano
brothers. Apparently they didn't much appreciate being
called "beaners." Live and learn.

But that eased up after a while, and the little Brown-Shirts-in-training learned to leave me be. There was really only one Skin who caught and maintained my interest. Henry Fulson: fifteen years old, locked up for ethnic intimidation and vandalizing a black-owned restaurant.

"Hey Mikal, we can resurrect the Fifth Reich. You and me. The time is now."

"I don't think so, Henry."

To this day I never fully deduced the origin of that kid's enthusiasm for the White Power movement and his dedication to fascism in general. But he was definitely devoted. It was a commitment to which even I could not relate.

"Hey Mikal. Have you read *The Turner Diaries?*"

"Of course."

"Awesome, ain't it?"

"I think the prose is kinda clunky, actually."

I had at that time developed a growing interest in writing. I read everything I could get my hands on, kept a notebook with me all hours of the day to write down memories, impressions, little bits of thoughts and recollections—some of which ended up in this very book. Henry was really excited by this, as he hoped I was penning a manifesto of some sort.

"Hey Mikal. Do you think, if Richard Lovecraft was alive—"

"*Were* alive."

"Were alive today he would have let me run with you guys? I can stomp like no one else. Yids, niggers, gooks—as soon as I'm free again the rampage begins."

"No, Henry, I don't think Richard would have welcomed you."

"Hey Mikal. How come?"

"Because . . . dude . . . you're fucking *black*."

Wherever one might fall in the spectrum of racial politics, it should be universally agreed upon that self-hatred of that magnitude can only bring about an ill conclusion. I have to hold to that. One morning at breakfast I tried explaining that to Mr. Fulson. This is how he replied:

"Hey Mikal. Look at this."

He pulled down the collar of his shirt and pointed to a discolored patch of pink skin about the size of a silver dollar right below his neckline.

"That's vitiligo, Henry. It's a skin disorder."

"No. You're wrong. That's the *white trying to come out*."

"Okay man . . ."

"Hey Mikal."

"Yeah?"

"Sieg heil!"

"Yeah."

EVEN IN DEATH RICHARD cast a shadow. And I wanted out of it. I'd loved him like a brother, no doubt, for whatever it was worth. I wanted no part of his ghost. I studied hard in juv, got my grades in good shape, and earned my GED while still in lockdown. Although I never consciously sought to leave behind the person that I had been, it subconsciously became my abiding purpose all the same. *Goodbye and good riddance to me.*

I SAW THE LAST shroud of that life fall away one night in lockdown, a week before my eighteenth birthday. I sat in rec watching TV when the local news came on. I was just about to leave when I saw a familiar face appear on the screen, standing before a judge begging for leniency: *Father of the Year*, my Suzi's favorite daddy. Seems his beloved daughter had decided one day that all that love and affection was more than she could bear, so she took his gun out of the sock drawer, locked herself in the bathroom, and emptied out the contents of her skull all over the tiles. When asked by the judge why he felt he should receive mercy from the court he replied, "Because I've already been handed the worst punishment of all. The loss of my daughter. *More* than a daughter, really."

Three bailiffs had to tackle Suzi's mother and drag her from the courtroom screaming. Then they cut back to the *tsk*ing anchorfolk and a commercial break and I don't suppose anyone else really cared. And that was that.

SOMETIMES, LATE AT NIGHT, when I'm the only person in the apartment awake and my vertigo is so severe that all I can do is lie on the floor and cover my head, I'll hear that woman screaming deep in my mind. *Shhhhhhh, Ma. Not so loud.*

GO TO SLEEP, SUZE. *Sleep tight, hon.*

"Mikal, let's pretend like we're going to get married someday, okay?"

Sure thing, sweetheart. Anything you want.

I COULDN'T HAVE SAVED her.

BUT, YOU KNOW, I coulda tried.

TWENTY-SEVEN

"Mikal. Psssst, Mikal. Ya know sump'n?"

"Hey Kaleb. What's goin' on, buddy?"

"Look at my knee. It's all skinned up."

"That's pretty badass, dude."

"Go long. I'll frow you the ball to you."

"Gimme a hug first."

I go to squeeze him but he's just made of water and now he's gone and my shirt's all wet and I wake up crying with blood dripping from my nose and I hope to god I wasn't talking in my sleep.

"You okay, babe?" Darcy asks. She rolls over and hugs me from behind, tosses my hair out of the way, and kisses my neck.

"Yeah. It's just . . . sinuses . . . allergies . . ." I wipe the line of blood onto my hand and lick it off so she's none the wiser.

Life after juvie was not much but a series of shit jobs for quite a while, each louder and hotter than the one before: kitchens, factories, roofing, asphalt. Three-odd years passed without my recognition. I was on autopilot. Numb. Maintaining an open-door policy on friendships kept me in places to stay as I shuffled from job to job, apartment to apartment, often living with groups of guys fresh from the joint who had done much harsher time than I. But they accepted me as a fellow ex-con and that's just the way it was. Often I was the only white. What can you do? *How did I come full circle?*

With few additional expenses I put aside a couple of bones every month for ink work. I had a lot to cover up, and opted for mostly black and red tribal vines and shading to mask the crude bluish stains I'd come to loathe. You can still make out the swastika over my heart today if I point it out, but it's as gone as I could hope for.

DON'T ASSUME I HAD turned any leaves or corners. Nope. I was the same person I'd ever been, *whomever that was.* Quick to anger, quick to fight, I kept my tongue sharp and loose in case someone needed a cutting (and plenty did). Even to this day I don't *feel* appreciably different. And of course I've left a string of frustrated, unsatisfied women in my wake.

"You're a fucking zombie, Mikal!" said *Whatshername.*

"I'm sorry, did you say something?"

Forever alone in a crowd. I'd simply learned at last to accept and embrace that that's how I am and that's the way it is. I'm good on my own. Today, as I was in '96, I'm surrounded by friends. Always. Lucky that way. But I'm just fine on my own all the same. I'm not a soldier, I've never been a soldier, and no costume will ever make me one.

"Do you need to take something, Mike?" Darcy asks me. "Are you feeling dizzy?"

"No, I'm okay, hon. Go back to sleep."

I WAS DIAGNOSED WITH chronic positional vertigo. Thanks to repeated head and neck trauma, and some fairly nasty inner-ear damage, I'll likely have to deal with bouts of it for the rest of my life. It comes and goes, and it's not as bad these days as it once was. The headaches and nosebleeds have largely subsided as well. All I can say is, thank god for sweet Mary Jane. She keeps me sane. I don't smoke a lot, just a joint here, a bong hit there. But it helps me keep my balance and perspective.

AFTER SOME TIME HAD passed, I found myself becoming more and more cognizant of the damage I had been party to. The pointless violence, the *terrorism*. It would dawn on me in waves and spurts and I'd see in my mind the screaming, pleading face of someone I was about to smash.

"Please no. Please. Please don't, dear god!"

I'd wonder where they all were today, how they'd recovered, if they'd recovered at all. So much suffering I had caused so many people . . . it began to claw away at me. Devoured me from the inside out. I'd try for anger as an easy grab, putting the blame on them for whatever wrong I'd pretended that they had done. But that was fruitless.

"Say yer sorry, Mikal. Tell 'em yer sorry and you won't do it no more."

"How, Kaleb? Who do I tell?"

"Do yer punishment, Mikal."

"For how long?"

Drinking myself unconscious seemed like the right way to go. But all that did was render me unable to distinguish when the vertigo was on top of me and when it wasn't. And it turned me into my father. *Life ain't nothing but listening to other people fuck and watching other people die . . .*

There was no penance I could do . . . there's none now . . . there never will be.

"I'M SORRY . . . SOMEBODY hear that I'm sorry . . ."

SOMETIME LATE INTO 1998 I began gradually making my way toward Columbus where, without fully realizing why, I would find myself at community activist meetings organized by students from OSU. My lifelong interest in environmental concerns lead me to ECO and Corporate Watch and other grassroots organizations whose mission it was to monitor what Big Business was shitting out all over us. Neighborhood cleanup projects in low-income areas also became an abiding concern.

IT WAS AT ONE of these meetings that I met Darcy. She was so unlike any of the girls from my past. Soft and light and kind of rounded. Quick-witted, compassionate, intelligent. Delicate, but not the least bit fragile. I remember seeing her first as she held the conch about staging a demonstration on campus. About . . . something or other. I've forgotten her words today, but I remember she was a pretty terrible public speaker and no one really listened to her. She's not a commanding presence, and I love her for that. Seeing her try to hold the attention of a room full of people and having them all but ignore her, I knew she'd be my wife someday. Her shoulders are unburdened. Her eyes are uncluttered, and I don't think she's ever really known any deep or lasting pain. I love her for that. There is nothing pointy or jagged about her. She's soft and rounded. I hope, if and when she ever reads this book, it doesn't upset her too much. I'd rather she didn't read it at all.

DARCY'S FAMILY ARE OLD-MONEY Taxachusetts liberals. They're very *nice* people and I mean that in all its benign blandness. Sometimes I wonder if they live on the same planet as the rest of us. It's rarefied air they breathe, and it'd be useless for me to ever argue with them or try to tell them where I've been. They'd be sickened. Rightfully so, I suppose. But they've accepted this tatted-up white-trash hooligan into their clan with open arms, so I'm certainly grateful. In fact it was Darcy's father who helped me apply for the Appalachian scholarship that enabled me to attended Ohio State. Full ride. I'd likely have never gone otherwise. Darcy and I both graduate this year, she with a degree in Poli-Sci, me in Creative Writing. For whatever that's worth. It's more than I could have ever hoped for and a good piece better than I deserve.

"I wish you'd quit saying that," Darcy says. "You're a good person and you work hard."

I'm glad you don't know me, sweetheart. I hope you never do.

I'M HOLDIN' LIKE CAULFIELD, you see. I'm here to catch her. I need to protect her from gargoyles like me.

I TRY TO GO back to sleep, but my baby brother has morphed into D'antre Philips who has morphed into my father who has morphed into Suzi's father who has morphed into Vice President Dick Cheney who is shooting fire and napalm out of his cock porno style, and I might as well wake up. That decision is clinched when a one-hundred-fifty-pound sack of hair and muscle lands on me from nowhere and I'm slapped repeatedly in the face with a large slab of hot bologna.

"Igor! Gah! Off the bed!"

The mammoth German shepherd growls in protest and continues to lick me about the chin.

"He just wants to love ya," my wife murmurs half-asleep. "Doncha, Doodlebug?" She coos, "Yessss him doessss."

"Jesus! What the fuck did he roll in?"

"You don't want to know." And back to dreamland she goes.

———————

SO I GET UP to go to my den, maneuvering through the gauntlet of sleeping bodies once again. Igor pushes my friend Daron off the futon and hunkers down next to Daron's boyfriend, Chang. Chang scratches Igor's chest and the mutant beast happily kicks his leg in the air.

"Hey don't mind me," Daron says, rubbing his boney, carpet-burned elbows. "I'm fine here on the floor, ya dig?"

And all is right with the world. I'm very fortunate to have the circle of friends I have these days. As crowded as my apartment is right now, I'm glad that they're all here. A religious person might say that I'm *blessed.* I'd simply say that the fates have been charitable, if not fair.

Interesting group assembled here. For as young and diverse as we all are, there are a lot of skeleton-packed closets amongst us. I think my wife may be the only person in this apartment tonight with no grim secrets or heavy baggage. I love her for that.

DARON FOLLOWS ME TO the den. He packs a bowl with some particularly sticky green and I hit Random on my CD player. It's a *tragic* mix tonight. All music by bands who've had members die violent deaths. Pantera. Joy Division. Acid Bath. Stigmata Dog. Run-DMC. *Good times.*

"How's the book comin', yo?" Daron asks, choking out a cloud of smoke. "Am I in it?"

"You are now," I say as he hands me the glass pipe.

"Always meant to write a book."

"So do it. Write about your times on the road. Although . . . I guess that's kinda been done, huh?"

"Yeah. All I got is poetry . . . and I hate books of poetry, ya dig?"

"I guess."

"So hey, we gotta celebrate this weekend, right? You and your better half are gradumagatin', Shay got a job, and it's coming up on Chang's and my anniversary. Four years, yo, can you dig that?"

Daron and Chang have been underground since the beginning of the millennium. Their fingerprints are on a couple of fairly high-profile piles of rubble, and they've rubbed shoulders with a rather frightening array of militants, destroyers, and unstable misfits. *But, of course, that's all in the past, right? Sure it is.* Although still devoted and die-hard left-wing radicals, they've since denounced violence wholesale and are heartily committed to complete pacifism. Admire that though I may (and I don't really know how I feel about it), I can't truthfully say the same for me. And despite the millions of dollars in property damage they've been party to, there's never been an injury or death as a result. I, of course, once again, cannot say the same.

"All that shit's over and done with, yo," Daron says. "Chang and me, we're just a bitchy old couple nowadays, right?"

"And if the shit goes down you can say it was all Chang's fault anyway. Heh heh."

"No doubt, man. I'm innocent, ya dig? Course I gotta be grateful to my baby. If I'da never met him I'd be just another Midwestern faggot married to a fat girl." We laugh.

"All right, get the fuck out. I got work to do."

"Your devil dog pushed me outta bed."

"As skinny as you and Chang are, there's plenty of room on that futon. Or you can sleep on the couch with Shayla."

"Dig, you know I love Shay. But I'm not trying to lay that close to a *female*, right?" He gives an affected shudder and I chuck a rubber dog toy at him. He runs off with a squeal.

Shayla is another dear friend from the wrong side of the law. A runaway since she was eleven, my girl whored until she was fifteen. That makes me sad. But she's one of the toughest people I've ever known. After my wife, Shayla is my favorite person in the whole world. Darcy would likely say, "After Shayla, Mikal is my favorite person in the whole world." That's just the way it is.

There's a select few people who give off a great, shining light. The rest of us can only bask, or burn, blistering, blinded, trying to dance in it.

I think Shay is one of those people. It's hard not to be drawn to her. And it's hard to know how to feel. I promised myself to purge those folks from my life. But at the end of the day, we're all just giant moths compelled by the light. That's just the way it is.

AND IN FACT, SPEAK o' *de debbil*, here she is right now, reading over my shoulder as I'm trying to write.

"I ain't readin' over yo' damn shoulda. I'm just lookin'. Hey, and don't be typin' ever'thang I be sayin'. I don't talk like 'at anyhow. Uh! You ain't right!"

She sits down in the purple beanbag chair and sticks out her tongue at me. I cackle all Snidely Whiplash.

"You ain't right, Mikal," she says again.

"I ain't left either."

"How come you write my name as *Shayla?*"

"It's pretty, don't you think?"

"Yeah, I like it a real lot. But you can use my real name if you want to. You almost finished?"

"I think so."

"I want to read it."

"I'll give you a copy. Promise."

The music plays a bit too loud for this time of night/ morning. Shayla rocks out to Pantera's "By Demons Be Driven," banging her head and throwing the horns.

"Beckon the call . . . beckon the call . . ."

"Work it, girl," I say.

"Love that stuff!"

"You nervous about starting work?"

"Yeah. It's funny. All the shit I done for money befo', and I'm scared of working at a bookstore."

"Yeah . . ." It makes me sad when she brings that up. But the past has passed. I hope.

"It's cool, though."

"Just take it as it comes."

"I done *that* already," she laughs.

"Not what I meant."

"Ai'ight, Mikey-Mike," she yawns. "I'm goin' back to sleep. G'night."

But I know she's not going to sleep just yet. It's the same routine every time. She says "G'night," then she goes to the kitchenette and puts on a pot of coffee for me. Sure enough, I hear the bean grinder right now.

I THINK ABOUT THE Mikal who appears in this book. Mikal The Bald. Mikal the Holy Warrior, skinny and scum tatted, sleeping in combat boots, *cuz you just never know when you gotta kick somebody*. I still have his boots around here somewhere. I try not to imagine what he would do to the people in this apartment if he were to walk in here right now. *Nothing, if he was by himself. But with his army . . . with his army . . .*

SHAYLA PLACES A STEAMING mug of pure Colombian heaven on my desk and flips the disc changer to Stigmata Dog.

"That oriental girl is so wild-lookin'," she says, looking at the CD's inlay card. "The vocalist. Pearl Harbor."

"She's Japanese. It's funny. At first I assumed she was a man. Or a young boy anyway."

"What ever happened to this group?"

"Bus accident. About three or four years ago. She and a guitar player survived, barely, rest of the band went splat on the highway. Not far from here really. Just north."

"That's how rock stars go out, ain't it?"

"Just the way it is." I lift the mug to my lips and take a cautious sip. Perfect.

"I know you like yo' coffee like you like yo' women," she says. "Hot and creamy with two lumps of sugar."

"I do like my coffee like I like my women. Cold, black, and bitter."

"You so *wrawng*," she groans, twisting my greasy, unwashed hair into a braid. "It ain't a braid," she says. "It's a *fishbone*. Four ropes instead of three."

"I see."

She hugs me goodnight from behind and turns to exit.

"I'mma give poor Daron the couch so he ain't gotta sleep on the flo'."

"Score!" We hear Daron shout and he dives onto the couch.

"Cool if I go sleep with Darcy?"

"You're gonna sleep with *my wife*?"

If a black girl could blush, she does.

"You *triflin'*! I mean, y'know, sleep in your bed. You ain't goin' back to sleep, I know that. You won't sleep for another three days 'n shit. Ain't nothin' funny goin' on."

"I think it's funny."

"Ugh. Good night, Mister Triflin'-ass. Oh hey, I forgot to tell you, some girl named Sherry called for you. Said she'd call back."

And she does.

"Mikal?"

Well I'll be damned . . .

"Hey Sherry. Long time."

"Wow. Yeah. God, you sound different."

"Nine years."

"So you got my letter."

"I did, yes."

"What time is it in Ohio?"

"Sun's coming up."

"Is it too late to talk?"

I tell her of course not.

BUT . . . MAYBE IT is. It is too late. Too late in our lives. Too late in the game. *Nine years*. We try to play catch up. But she doesn't really want to talk about her life today and I don't want to talk about mine. We banter in vague *nothingmuch* for a while, then simply sit in silence, piling up long-distance minutes.

"So . . . um . . . thanks for writing back," I say. "That was a big help. And I really enjoyed, you know, getting your side of things. It was . . . illuminating."

"Did you makes any changes?"

"Well, I kinda . . . tightened some screws. Or some . . . bolts."

"Okay . . . but were you honest?"

"Tried to be. But I don't know. You know? I mean, is that even possible?"

"I don't know. Maybe not."

"Maybe my memory lies."

"Maybe mine does too. Are you using my real name?"

"Do you want me to?"

"Up to you. You're the writer, you make the decisions. We're all in your hands now, Mikal. You write the history, you control our fates. You're the boss. That's what you always wanted, isn't it?"

No . . .

"I don't open the can of worms, Sher, I just kick it over."

"Fair enough."

"Tell me something."

"Hey look, it's been great to talk to you, but I gotta go."

"Hold up a minute."

"Mikal, I've told you all I can."

"Just tell me . . . Did you stay together?"

"What?"

"You and Niani. Was it . . . true love and all that horseshit?"

"I'm . . . very happy today. Portland's—"

"Are you still *together*?"

"You haven't let go, Mikal, have you?"

"Yes I have. What's done is done. But . . . I just can't help but think that . . . that if you two stayed together, then at least it wasn't all . . . pointless."

"Mikal . . ."

"Just tell me, all right?"

"This is more of your *destiny* bullshit. Fate and whatnot. I don't believe in it. Life is chaos, Mikal. It doesn't mean anything."

"That's not very Catholic of you."

"Fuck no, it's not. And thank god, or whatever, that I left that rubbish behind. It's all random. Period."

"No, it's not. We have free will to choose our paths, but the paths themselves are set."

"One big Choose Your Own Adventure story, huh?"

"That's a pretty . . . simplistic way to put it, but yeah."

"You still love him, don't you."

"What?"

"You're trying to make his death mean something. You want it to matter. Well it does. Okay? It does. But only for its own sake."

"No. Listen—"

"You still don't know who you are, do you, Mikal?"

"That's not fucking it! Sherry . . . listen to me. At least if you two were really *meant* for each other, then—"

"Then what? Nothing I tell you is going to satisfy you. I-I can't . . . I can't let you open up any more hurts in me, Mikal." She starts to cry. "I'm all cut up again. Nine years! Nine years. I don't blame you, and I'm glad I was able to help you, but I can't do this anymore. I thought I had healed over, but I'm bleeding again. And you are too. You've got to stop bleeding, Mikal. Let's not do this to ourselves."

"Just tell me. Tell me and it's over with. It'll be done. Forever."

"It's over with now. I wish you nothing but the best"—*sniff*—"I really do. And I, I'll be watching the bookshelves for your name. I sure will. Take care of yourself. Okay? Write your ending, Mikal. It's yours to write."

And with that she hangs up. I check the caller ID. Unlisted.

Just as well.

I PACE A BIT. Turn the music off. Light a joint. *Wish I had some black rock.* Igor moseys in and headbutts me in the thigh. I rub him behind his ears. I catch my own reflection in the full mirror hanging on the wall and undo the fishbone. I'm shirtless. My viney, abstract faux-tribal tattoos weave all about my arms and torso. I'm not as skinny as the boy in the book. Not anymore. My hair hangs in greasy strands down my back. I can't even read the look in my own eyes. Colder than they feel in my head. Rather dull. Lifeless. I may not know who I am . . . but I know who I look like.

WRITE YOUR ENDING, MIKAL. *It's yours to write.*
FIN
DAS ENDE
THAT'S JUST THE WAY IT IS
THE END

AFTERWORD

L ord, spare me from any more Blackchurch funerals.

IT'S BEEN A WHILE since I've written anything here. Life
has soldiered on, as it is wont to do. My friends have all hit
the road once more and I'm alone again. Naturally. I miss
them all of course, and I look forward to seeing them again at
some point . . . but *these* are good times. On-my-own times.
Even my wife is off visiting old high school chums in Boston.
And, due to some sort of electromagnetic gravity pull science
has yet to fully explain, I'm back in Blackchurch.

The place is thick with ghosts and phantoms this weekend. I've brought Igor down to see my folks, as he's probably
the closest they'll ever come to having a grandchild.

It's Monday afternoon as I write and I'm packing up to
head back to Columbus. Yesterday was funeral day as it often
is in Blackchurch. The host and guest of honor for Sunday's
affair was a chap named Rakeem Hollis who had recently run
afoul of local law enforcement. Apparently said police felt
that sixty nightstick blows to the skull were necessary to convince Mr. Hollis that he had the right to remain silent. I didn't
really know Rakeem, but I attended the funeral for my mom's

sake, who attended for the sake of Rakeem's mother, Yolanda. The Hollises live across the street and over one. Dad came as well, but bitched about all the "Blackchurch voodoo and ooga-booga." He's referring, of course, to the screaming, fainting, and general bedlam of African American funerals. I have to admit, it's a little hard for me to take as well. But that's just the way it is. You really can't beat the music, though. It does give the spirit a good washing, for whatever that's worth.

I felt as suitably out of place in church as I do in 'Church. As well I should. Scanning about the room I looked for familiar faces. Trey McKinley was there with a very pregnant blonde. Ezekial Johnson and his parents sat in the third pew on the right side, and I held to some strange hope that maybe Niani would join them. It was in vain. *Just as well.*

Sitting there as people cried all around me and some fat, sweaty preacher said something or other about God welcoming his child home and choirs of angels and whatnot, I felt that it wasn't just Rakeem's funeral I was attending just then. It was all the funerals I should have attended and didn't.

Sleep tight. Sleep tight.

The choir sang:

"And he will raise you up on eagle's wings / bear you on the breath of dawn / make you to shine like the sun . . ."

It occurred to me that I could have dressed a little nicer. Then it occurred to me that, no, I could not have. This beaten old blue suit is the best that I own. Just the way it is. And fat preacher-man said something about one day all of God's children will sit together at the banquet table under the banner of God's love. Or words to that effect.

"Bullshit on a stick," muttered my dad.

"Amen," I said. *Amen.*

AFTER THE SERVICE EVERYONE milled about out on the sidewalk for a very long time. I could tell my dad was getting antsy, eager to get away from this throng of Negroes and home to his gin bottle. Tanya delivered all the necessary hugs and condolences, and they headed home. No telling why, but I decided to stick around and told them I'd join them later.

Eventually those of us who remained all marched down Churchwalk to the cemetery. Some folks sang:

"Sometimes I feel / like a motherless child / a long way from home . . ."

THERE AT THE GRAVE site folks mumbled more prayers. More singing, more consoling, but I can't be sure that I was really there. I felt like an observer, at least one step removed. *This is a sad show. Somebody change the channel.* Rakeem's grandmother fell backwards wailing and a little girl threw dandelions into the grave.

"Tiesha, you stop that," her mother said. "You leave Rakeem alone. He sleepin'."

SLEEP TIGHT RAKEEM . . .

I FINALLY GOT UP the gumption to approach Trey McKinley and his pregnant lady friend. *He's still a little scarred up about the face.*

"Trey McKinley," I said, my voice shaking more than I anticipated. "It's been a while. How you doin'?"

Trey turned his head with a questioning look. "Uh, hi." He shook my hand. "Have we met?"

"Long, long time ago. I'm Will and Tanya Fanon's son. Mike. I live in Columbus. But, um, hey, I just wanted to say . . . that . . . *I'm sorry.*"

"Thank you. I appreciate that. Rakeem was my dude. He'll be missed."

"Yeah. Yeah. I just wanted to tell you . . . how sorry I am."

"Cool. Take it easy, Mike. Church."

"Church."

TIME TO GO. MISSION *accomplished. One step at a time. Time to go . . .* But not before *that voice* sneaked up behind me.

"How 'boutcha, whiteboy." *How 'bout me.* "I been wantin' to talk at you for a minute, Mikal." Against my stronger instincts I turned around slow and casual. *I will be damned.* "You recognize me, bruh?"

Goddamn . . .

"Sure. Yeah. How could I forget?" He hadn't aged a day. We shook hands. "How, um, how ya been, D'antre?"

"Been better. I'm tired of buryin' my niggas, ya heard?"

"Sure."

"This be my third funeral in two months, son. I ain't havin' no more of it."

"That's hard."

"You know how it is, buryin' your friends."

"Yeah . . ."

"I done read your manuscript."

Fuck . . .

"Zat right?"

"Whatcha say you 'n' me grab us some drinks down at the Soul Lounge. I'm buyin'."

"Wouldn't say no."

IF YOU LOOK UP "ghetto dive" in any respectable dictionary you will find a picture of the Soul Lounge. It's a tavern stuck in time, replete with dark, life-beaten, yellowed-eyed characters who are also stuck in time. They don't take credit cards, the jukebox is stocked with 78s, and if you'd like to sit in the nonsmoking section you'll be pointed in the direction of the broom closet. Good times.

Turns out D'antre had acquired a copy of the manuscript through Shayla. He'd been up in Columbus doing a drop-in book signing for *Princess Africa Jones* at the shop where Shayla was working. They became fast friends and she even stayed in Blackchurch for a while. I had lost touch with her by that time, and the last D'antre heard she had headed off for Baton Rouge, Louisiana. I'm kind of sad about that, and I hope I get a chance to see her again someday.

"Guess shit got a little fiery between y'all, eh? You an' and Shay an' your old lady."

"I don't want to talk about it," I told him. He nodded and ordered us two Wild Turkeys on the rocks.

"Tell me somethin'. The first time we 'met,' or whatever you'd call it, did I really say to you 'Welcome to Niggatown'?"

"If I'm lyin' I'm dyin'," I said.

"That's funny."

"Why's it funny?"

"I just think it's funny. I don't remember that at all. I do remember poor lil Artiz gettin' shot up."

"*Artiz*. Huh. I always wondered, whatever happened to him?"

"He survived, but he got a bad blood infection, son. Nasty shit. The head shot did him no favors neither, ya heard. He done been in a wheelchair ever since. And he don't talk too great. Here: a toast." We raised our tumblers. "To absent friends."

"To absent friends. Cheers."

"Mud in your eye."

"D'antre, man, before we go any further with all this, I just want you to know that . . . I'm not the person I used to be. All right? So whatever you might be thinking after read—"

"Hey," he shrugged. "Who is, ya heard?"

"Right. Right."

"I was feelin' your story, dawg. Believe dat. And it got me thinkin' . . . bout lookin' at my own self, ya heard. It's hard puttin' your friends in the ground, ya feel me. Hard. It's hard when they die . . . but in a way I think it's harder when they kill, right? I've had both, knahmsayin, just like you. It's harder when they kill and they live cuz in a way it's like they are dead to you now, or half dead, but you still gotta hang with they ghost and perp like ain't nothin' wrong."

"I know what you mean. It's hard to know how to feel."

"It's hard to know how to feel. Dead up. Before Rakeem, the last cat I had to bury, we was real close, ya heard. I had mad love for him like a brother, knamean, but he done some *ill shit*. Just wrong shit, son. All fucked up in his head, a soldier ya heard, a vet, all fucked up with the gov'ment's poison . . . And when they finally brung him down, cuz they had to . . . I was . . . relieved. And I got hatred for myself for that. At least he died free, whatever that's worth."

"Yeah . . ."

I bought us another round. We sat in silence for a long time. When he spoke again, it was a completely different voice. Clear, precise, almost mannered.

"You know, Mikal, it's a peculiar thing," he said. "I'm staring down the barrel of forty years old. It seems like I should have found my *space* by now. But I feel like an alien. That's how it is. These past couple of years I've been renting an apartment in an old converted church. THE church, the big one, the original *Blackchurch*, on the corner of Blackstone and Desmond."

"Churchwalk."

"Churchwalk, yes. Heart of the neighborhood. The namesake, for chrissake."

"Dude, I saw that! I saw it when we were walking down to the cemetery. You live there? There's police tape all around it."

"They converted it some years ago to a community hall,

bingo and theater and whatnot, and there's a little apartment for rent on the second floor, and that's what I've called home for the past couple of years. Hoo boy. Thirty-six years old, a published author, and I'm living like the hunchback of Notre Dame." We laughed. He shrugged, matter-of-fact. "And now, thanks to my boy, RIP, and his demons, there's police tape around it and blood on the inside."

"Damn, that's one of those moments when you gotta step back and take inventory, right?"

"Yeah, so let's see: most of my friends since childhood are either felons or fertilizer. My wife and my baby girl moved away to Madison, Wisconsin . . ."

"I didn't know they even *let* black people live there."

"News to me too. I live in a bloodstained church with a devil-possessed blast furnace. And now . . . I'm sitting in a nigga-only ghetto bar with a cracker-ass neo-Nazi."

"Yep. Somebody took a wrong turn somewhere."

"And I think it's me."

I wasn't sure what to say. I'd always thought of D'antre Philips as the toughest, cockiest motherfucker in the world. *But here we are. He's got his small moments too.*

How did *we end up here? What kind of twist in the road did I miss? Maybe the paths aren't set after all. Maybe there are no paths. Maybe it is all random. Chaos . . . absolute freedom. I could learn to enjoy freedom on my side.*

"Well . . . ," I answered finally, breathing deep and coughing a bit on the stagnant Soul Lounge air. "There's really only one thing I can say about all that, my man."

"Yeah? What's that?"

"It's gonna make one HELLBOMBER of a book when you write it, son!"

We laughed heartily and clinked our glasses together.

"You goin' in my book, muthafucka," he cackled, his voice returning to "normal."

"Fair play to you," I replied. "You're in *mine*."

Just then the tavern door swung open and I noticed that evening had completely set in. Slumping in the door, stooped and limping on a cane, was a rough-looking peckerwood with stringy, shoulder-length hair. A graying, too-tight Judas Priest concert tee struggled to contain his rather sizable potbelly. Sleeving each arm was a mosaic of faded, undefined tattoos. This guy couldn't have been but thirty-three, but he looked *much* older.

"Ladies and gentleman," the bartender announced, "or *gentlemen* and gentlemen I guess . . . it is the one and only *Jack Curry*."

"'Bout time you faced the Devil," D'antre whispered to me. *Yeah . . . 'bout time . . .*

"D!" Jack shouted, hobbling over to us. "What's shakin', hard rhymer?"

"How you feelin', J playa?"

"Better than I look, I hope. How you holdin' it, dawg?"

"Tucked into my sock, ya heard." They embraced forcefully and Jack took a seat on the stool next to me. "We missed ya at the service, kid."

"I don't do funerals," Jack answered. "Fuck alla that, son. I don't do churches as a rule. The six-six-six on my skull starts pounding and glowing and shit. Keem knows I love him. And I know he's looking down on me from above. Every time I try to take a shit or strangle the sea serpent. Filthy bastard."

"Jack, this here is Mikal Fanon."

Curry turned to me, looked me right in the eyes and offered the glad hand.

"Good to meet you, Mikal," he said smiling warmly.

HOW DO YOU DO IT?

How do you drop twelve years of seething hatred all at once? How do you push it all aside? How do you control the wave of rage that crashes down on you? You don't. You don't drop it and you don't control it. But you *try*. Because you have to. I shook his hand and smiled back. And when I did there was no mistaking the bullet scars on both sides of his left wrist. Or the razor scars on his right.

"Um, yeah, good . . . uh . . . good to meet you too, Jack. Good to meet you too."

"Welcome to the ass-crack of the universe, dude."

"I've been up in it before."

"So what brings you to Blackchurch?"

"Mikal grew up here," D'antre said.

"Oh yeah?"

"Not exactly. I lived here from . . . for a minute. But I'm up in Slow-lumbus right now. Just graduated from OSU."

"Aw, that's hip man," Jack said, slapping me on the back. "That's killer. Good for you. Dontell!" he called to the barkeep. "Get this man a Maker's on the rocks. On me. Man, that's something I always wanted to do, you know. Graduate from college. I was really into learning foreign languages. Wanted to be an interpreter or a translator or something. I just really got into the idea of being able to communicate with lots of different folks. You know? Weeeell," he chuckled, "so much for that shit."

D'antre looked at me. I thought he might call me out, but he didn't.

"See, Jack did his time at Warren County," D'antre said with a smirk. "That's an easy piece."

"Yeah, *easy piece* is right, muhfucka," Jack replied, "Easy piece my ass. You try being a cripple in lockdown and tell me if the sun is shinin'."

"Boy," D'antre said, rolling his eyes, "with all the cousins and shit you got who are locked up in that joint, going to jail's like a family reunion." We all laughed.

"You done time, Mike?" Jack asked.

"Just juvie."

"Yeah, I did juvie."

"So did I," D'antre said. "Juv was the first place and time

I ever saw a dude jerk off another dude. I was all like, Y'ALL ARE SICK! and then I proceeded to spank it into a old sweat sock. Cuz, see, I got *standards*."

"Well," Jack said stoically, "as long as the sock was a chick—"

"The sock was yo' mama." The whole bar laughed at that, and Jack called Dontell over and bought another round. *Yo' mama* snaps are round-worthy in these parts.

We talked and drank the night away. Spent a good piece talking about our wives: D'antre's ex, Jack's soon-to-be ex, my Darcy. *Never-to-be ex*. I had the sudden urge to call her in Boston. Make sure she was okay. See if she could come home early because I missed her. *Must be the booze. Alone time is good time . . .*

At some point President George W. Bush appeared on the bar's decrepit black-and-white TV. A collective groan filled the room and grumbles of "white devil" were heard. Jack chucked a full basket of peanuts at the television.

"DIE YOU EVIL FUCK!!!" he shouted as the peanuts smashed against the screen and scattered all over the floor. No one so much as batted an eye. Dontell the bartender simply bent over and swept up the shells.

"So, Molotov," Jack turned to D'antre, cool and collected. "How's *Princess* selling, kid?"

"It ain't. Not really. Hedgehog Press got bought out by a larger publisher and they kinda don't know what to do with it."

"You writing something new?" I asked.

"Yeah."

"Is it about Blackchurch?" Jack asked.

"You know it."

"Sweet."

"Mikal's a writer too," D'antre said. "Just finished a book."

"F'real?"

"Well, it's not quite done," I said.

"I'd like to read it."

"Yeah. Okay. Sure."

AROUND 1:30 AM, AFTER stopping by my parents' place to collect Igor, we stumbled back down Blackstone Street to Jack's house (his mother's house, actually). There we were greeted by Jack's soon-to-be ex, Elaine, a quiet little hamster-faced girl with red hair and big hips. She seemed really nice and they appeared to be happy enough . . . but you can tell when a relationship is through, and theirs is most certainly over. That's just the way it is.

After gobbling up some delicious leftover potato salad Elaine had made for Rakeem's wake, Jack, D'antre and I sat out on the back porch, drinking cheap red wine, smoking equally cheap hash, and daring the sun to rise. Three young old criminals shaking our fists at the night. Igor wrestled happily in the backyard with Jack's three-legged pit bull Araya and we collectively ignored the persistent sound of gunfire and crying sirens.

About 3:00 AM D'antre went into the house to try to call Madison, Wisconsin. It seemed a bit late to be making phone calls, but he was determined to talk to his daughter right then and there was no point telling him not to. BBC came on the radio with a report about the torture American soldiers had committed in Iraq and Guantanamo Bay. Jack shut off the radio.

"I can't deal with any more *torture*," he said. "It weighs on my mind too much."

"I feel you," I said.

"You a Public Enemy fan, Mike?"

"Aw hell yeah," I lied. He dropped *Fear of a Black Planet* into the CD player. It was pretty damn awesome. "Hey man, that's too bad about you and Elaine."

"That's life," he shrugged. "You take it as it comes."

"She seems like a real cool chick."

"Yeah, she is. It's not her fault, man. I'm not an easy guy to deal with. I mean, I only work twenty hours a week, I live with my mother, and I spend most of the day listening to right-wing talk radio and screaming at the top of my lungs."

"Yeah, dude, that's pretty obnoxious."

"True that. I mean, I love her and all, but she can do better." He paused for moment, then said, "I *really* loved a girl one time. A long time ago."

"Yeah? What happened?"

"After I went to prison I never saw her again. That was my fault too."

"What do you mean?"

"I mean she wrote me like every other day. Came to visit me every week. But something always got in the way and she couldn't see me. I didn't want her to. There I was, with a big steel rod through my thigh. All gimped out and crippled, head shaved bald. That's no way to be."

"Yeah . . ."

"I never even wrote her back. Eventually she moved away. The letters kept coming for years and years, well after I got outta the joint, and I never replied. Most I didn't even open. Finally they stopped. I loved that girl. But she couldn't love me back."

"Oh."

"I mean, she *did* love me, but not the way I loved her. She couldn't."

"Queer, huh?"

"Yeah, I mean what can ya do? It's how she was wired. Even if she wasn't . . . it wouldn't have worked. We were like twins, you know? From alternate realities. We weren't lovers, but we were soul mates, if that makes any sense at all."

"Sure."

"I told somebody one time that there are just a few people in the world who give off a great, shining light. The rest of us can only bask or burn . . ."

"Blistering," I said, "blinded, trying to dance in it."

"Yeah," he said, looking at me askew.

"You still believe that?"

"I don't know. I think we're all fucked up and lost. All of us. Big or small. I mean look at Adolf Hitler. Yeah he was charismatic and yeah he had presence and rocked the stage like a true star, but when shit got hot he blew his own head off. He wasn't the man folks thought he was."

"I guess that's true."

"Lots of people were hung up on Niani. Lots. Men *and* women. They were *fascinated* by her. Thought she was a mystery or a puzzle to solve. But I knew her. She was just a girl. Beautiful, sure, and brilliant. Magnetic. But she was just a girl. A goofy, awkward, silly, clumsy girl. She never did her own dishes and she was always breaking shit by accident. And she could be a real prickly bitch sometimes. I was always cleaning up after her. But I guess . . . she always cleaned up after me too. God . . . I loved her."

"Whatever happened to her?"

"Last I heard she moved to Portland."

"Really?"

"That was a while ago. I don't know if she's still there. Wherever she is, I hope she's happy. I'm sure she is."

"Me too," I said. "Me too."

I AWOKE ON JACK Curry's couch sometime around 8:30 AM. D'antre was asleep in the easy chair. No one else was about. I woke up Igor, who grumbled in protest, and I hooked on his leash. We crept quietly out of the house and out into the bright Blackchurch morning.

Down we walked, street after street, past churches, gun shops, liquor stores, weave boutiques, pawn shops, "checks cashed no questions asked," and house after boarded-up house. Each looked to be—and probably should have been—condemned, but none were. All occupied. Some with two or more families. *That's Blackchurch.*

One block from Will and Tanya's place I once again stepped onto the moving carousel. It spun me around and I fell into a lamppost. My head twirled like a top as I slid down the pole to the sidewalk, Igor whimpering and licking my face.

"Hey boy!" I opened my jittery eyes and looked across the street at an ancient black man sitting on a stoop smoking a cigarette and drinking a bottle of Wild Irish Rose. He flashed me a toothless smile and raised his drink. "Juth go on home and thleep it off, y'hear? You'll be a'ight."

I smiled back and pulled myself upright, the vertigo already subsiding. "I'm better already," I said. He cackled loudly and gave me the thumbs-up.

BACK AT THE HOUSE I called Darcy in Boston right away. I expected to get the voice mail, but she answered on the first half ring.

"Mikal?"

"Hey sweetheart."

"Hey! How's the baby?"

"He ate a guy."

"Whole?"

"Yep."

"Cool."

"Yeah. How's everybody?"

"Good. Good. They're all asking after you."

"Give 'em all a kiss for me."

" 'Kay. I miss you. Sooooo much. I want to come home early. What do you think?"

"You read my mind, Darce."

"Cool. Yeah, it was great catching up with everybody and all. But you know, they're my past. I'm ready to say goodbye to the past. I'm ready to come home. It's time to leave the past where it belongs. My future's with you and that's where I want to be."

"I couldn't agree more."

"Can't wait to see you."

"Can't wait."

"I'm catching the first plane back to Columbus."

"I'll be there waiting."

"I may get impatient and parachute out."

"I'll be there to catch you."

"I love you, Mikal."

"Hurry home and prove it."

I'M READY TO SAY *goodbye to the past. Goodbye, The Past. Goodbye, Blackchurch. Goodbye, old ghosts. Haunt ya later sometime. Goodbye old Mikal, young Mikal, whomever you are. Goodbye and good riddance to me.*

AND THAT WAS THAT.